S T A R G Å T E

SG·1 ™

THE ULTIMATE VISUAL GUIDE

STARGÅTE

SG·1.

THE ULTIMATE VISUAL GUIDE

BY KATHLEEN RITTER

Contents

FOREWORD

If you've missed something along the way—no, if you've missed <u>anything</u> along the way—you have but to slide your fingers into the following pages, part them a full one hundred-and-eighty degrees and begin your dizzying journey through Kate Ritter's *Stargate SG-1: The Ultimate Visual Guide.*

By now most regular viewers of *Stargate* (the television show) know its origin (the movie) and, as regular viewers, can fairly well trace the path of the show's vast and variant history. The not-so-regular viewers to the series have the benefit of the internet, a multitude of reruns, and burgeoning DVD packages that ostensibly harbor the whole story and thus the ability to catch up or familiarize. And then we have the huddled masses of regular folk who have never seen *Stargate SG-1* and for whom I personally drone a quiet mantra: "Oh, whoa, oh no, what have we here…" (R.D.A., 2006).

To all categories of humanoid (alien and non-alien alike) I say: have a sweet gander at *Stargate SG-1: The Ultimate Visual Guide*, (U.V.G.). Newbie or pro, it will blow your socks away.

When I was but a wee lad, contemplating a continued life of laziness and inactivity, I lit upon an old friend in the name of John Symes, who, by life's design, was running the castle at MGM—he in turn introduced me to a couple of fellas, one of whom became a good friend in Brad Wright. I was presented with the pilot script for *Stargate SG-1* and was asked to sign on for a two-year stint as Kurt Russell's stand-in. With the promise of potentially rapid advancement in the company and, times being what they were, I said no. Then I was told by all my new friends to actually <u>read</u> the script. This was a new concept for me, one normally reserved for kids these days who seem to be perpetually fondling the tendrils of modernity. But heck, I really wasn't in the mood to cash it all in (it takes real energy to quit) and, times being what they were, I read. And thus the seed was sown.

From the beginning there was always more to the concept than met the third eye. Once the series found its legs, and subsequently its creative rhythm, it became painfully obvious that we were to be pleasantly mired in the oddly flavored webs of longevity. Out of the gate I recall suspecting enormous potential for the show. Story lines examined foreign life forms, life styles, and forms of life; with particular attention paid to the philosophical, political and spiritual underpinnings of any number of cultures, foreign and domestic. Our heroes made friends, our heroes made enemies. They traveled a lot, garnering enough frequent flyer miles to skin a cat and back again. The ultimate goal then is to assist our viewers in recognizing the great and grand possibilities of a sweeping acceptance of ALL races…throughout the universe and the whole, wide world.

What Kate Ritter has provided here in the U.V.G. is invaluable—astoundingly so. Her chronicling of the entity that is *Stargate SG-1* will set you on a path of insight and understanding. This book is an amazing accomplishment. The detail is scary. I personally have no realistic perspective from which to judge, but I've been around this *Stargate* thing a bit to know that Ms. Ritter has absolutely nailed it!!

Read, enjoy…talk amongst yourselves.
And Kate, very nicely done, my friend. Congratulations!!

Richard Dean Anderson

Richard Dean Anderson

STARGATE SG-1

The Stargate

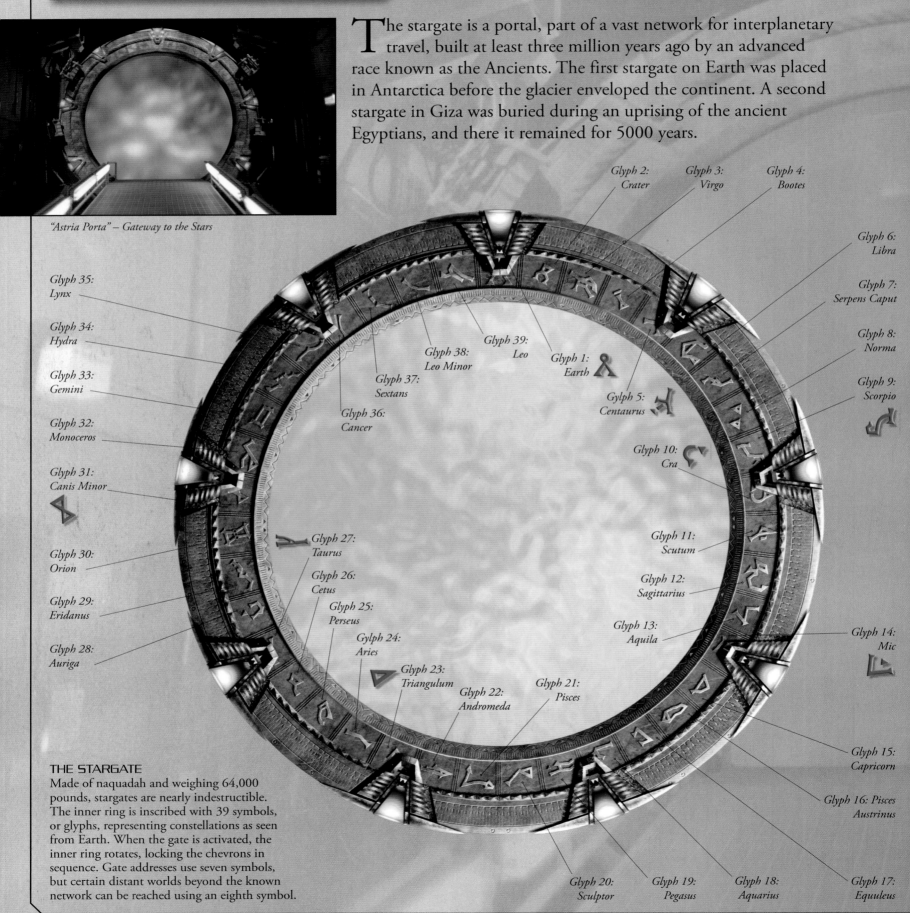

The stargate is a portal, part of a vast network for interplanetary travel, built at least three million years ago by an advanced race known as the Ancients. The first stargate on Earth was placed in Antarctica before the glacier enveloped the continent. A second stargate in Giza was buried during an uprising of the ancient Egyptians, and there it remained for 5000 years.

"Astria Porta" – Gateway to the Stars

Glyph 2:
Crater

Glyph 3:
Virgo

Glyph 4:
Bootes

Glyph 6:
Libra

Glyph 7:
Serpens Caput

Glyph 8:
Norma

Glyph 9:
Scorpio

Glyph 35:
Lynx

Glyph 34:
Hydra

Glyph 39:
Leo

Glyph 38:
Leo Minor

Glyph 1:
Earth

Glyph 33:
Gemini

Glyph 37:
Sextans

Glyph 5:
Centaurus

Glyph 32:
Monoceros

Glyph 36:
Cancer

Glyph 10:
Cra

Glyph 9:
Scorpio

Glyph 31:
Canis Minor

Glyph 30:
Orion

Glyph 27:
Taurus

Glyph 11:
Scutum

Glyph 29:
Eridanus

Glyph 26:
Cetus

Glyph 12:
Sagittarius

Glyph 25:
Perseus

Glyph 13:
Aquila

Glyph 28:
Auriga

Gylph 24:
Aries

Glyph 14:
Mic

Glyph 23:
Triangulum

Glyph 22:
Andromeda

Glyph 21:
Pisces

Glyph 15:
Capricorn

Glyph 16: Pisces
Austrinus

Glyph 20:
Sculptor

Glyph 19:
Pegasus

Glyph 18:
Aquarius

Glyph 17:
Equuleus

THE STARGATE

Made of naquadah and weighing 64,000 pounds, stargates are nearly indestructible. The inner ring is inscribed with 39 symbols, or glyphs, representing constellations as seen from Earth. When the gate is activated, the inner ring rotates, locking the chevrons in sequence. Gate addresses use seven symbols, but certain distant worlds beyond the known network can be reached using an eighth symbol.

Ernest Littlefield

HISTORY

In 1928 the stargate was recovered from beneath the sands of Egypt. Dr. Langford led the team which later conducted experiments on the artifact, but when the gate was activated manually in 1945 and Ernest Littlefield was lost through the portal, the program was abruptly shut down. By 1969, the gate was all but forgotten until Catherine Langford resumed her father's research. The stargate was moved to Cheyenne Mountain where its successful activation led to the first stargate mission to Abydos. More than a year later, in 1997, the stargate had once again been abandoned until the arrival of Apophis through the gate prompted the President to establish Stargate Command.

COMPOSITION

Despite the extraordinary complexity of stargate technology, it is possible to build a simple stargate that will dial only once, using materials available online, including 100 pounds of pure raw titanium, 200 feet of fiber-optic cable, seven 100,000-watt industrial-strength capacitors—and a toaster.

Orlin built a makeshift stargate.

WORMHOLE ARC

A power surge aimed at an outgoing stargate will cause the wormhole to jump, or "arc," to a different destination. The phenomenon first occurred when an unintentional weapons surge on P4A-771 caused an incoming wormhole to leap from the default SGC gate to the beta stargate in Antarctica.

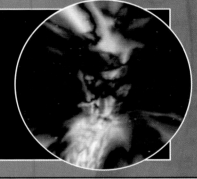

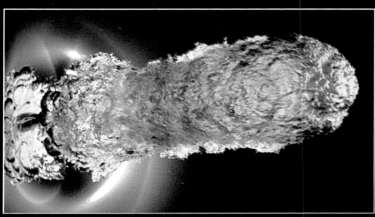
The initial kawoosh forms an event horizon of quantum particles.

WORMHOLE PHYSICS

Stargates are giant superconductors that absorb energy directly in many forms. As the inner wheel spins, the chevrons lock the address symbols into place and an artificial wormhole forms between two open gates, transferring an energized matter stream along an extra-dimensional conduit within a subspace field. The wormhole travels in only one direction, however certain kinds of energy including radiation, gravity, and radio transmissions, can be sent back through an outgoing wormhole. The kawoosh, or initial unstable vortex of gate activation, stabilizes to form the water-like effect of the event horizon.

Stepping through the event horizon allows instantaneous interplanetary travel.

BETA STARGATE

A second stargate was discovered on Earth, buried deep in an Antarctic crevasse about 50 miles outside of McMurdo Station. It was referred to as the beta stargate, however evidence suggests that it was in fact the original stargate on Earth, predating the Antarctic glacier. Although the beta stargate was officially decommissioned, it was secretly used by rogue NID teams for covert off-world missions before being sealed and returned to Area 51. When SG-1 became trapped aboard Thor's Asgard ship, they transported the alpha gate from the SGC aboard the ship to make their escape. The gate was lost when the ship crashed into the Pacific, but was recovered by the Russians and used briefly from their facility in Siberia. The beta gate was moved from storage to the SGC and remained in use until Anubis used an off-world weapon that threatened to detonate the gate and destroy Earth. The beta gate was removed from the SGC, launched into space on the X-302, and sent into a hyperspace window where it exploded over 3 million miles away. Through a negotiated agreement with the Russians, the original alpha stargate was returned to the SGC.

The Beta Stargate

RUSSIAN STARGATE

The Russians established a short-lived stargate program using the alpha stargate recovered from the Pacific.

EGYPT

Ra used the stargate near Giza in Egypt to establish his power base on Earth.

CHAAPA'AI

Chaapa'ai is the name used to refer to the stargate in the language of the Goa'uld.

The Stargate

T HE DIAL HOME DEVICE, or DHD, functions as both a power source and as a means of controlling the stargate. From its 38 symbols, a gate address is dialed by pressing a sequence of six symbols to identify a point in space, followed by a point of origin. Dialing seven symbols chosen from a pool of 38 non-repeating candidates results in about 63 billion possible stargate addresses.

DHD

The Egyptian DHD was discovered by the Germans in 1906, and therefore was missing from the original dig at Giza in 1928. It was confiscated by the Russians following World War II, and later loaned to the SGC and accidentally destroyed. The energy source of the Antarctic DHD was depleted shortly after its recovery. There is currently no functioning DHD on Earth.

Dial Home Device

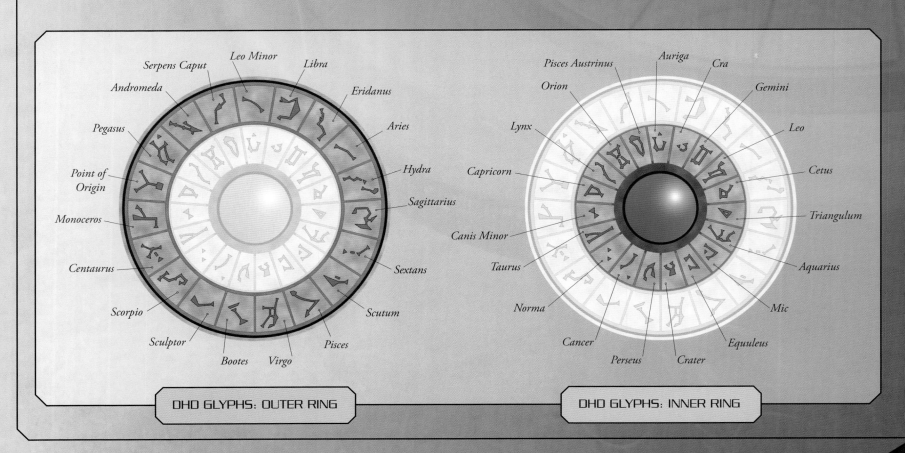

DHD GLYPHS: OUTER RING

Andromeda
Serpens Caput
Leo Minor
Libra
Eridanus
Pegasus
Aries
Point of Origin
Hydra
Monoceros
Sagittarius
Centaurus
Sextans
Scorpio
Scutum
Sculptor
Pisces
Bootes
Virgo

DHD GLYPHS: INNER RING

Pisces Austrinus
Auriga
Cra
Orion
Gemini
Lynx
Leo
Capricorn
Cetus
Canis Minor
Triangulum
Taurus
Aquarius
Norma
Mic
Cancer
Equuleus
Perseus
Crater

DIALING COMPUTER

Although the stargate was designed to use the DHD as a power source and control mechanism, it is possible to activate the gate using an alternate dialing system. Because the Giza stargate had been recovered without a DHD, it took 15 years and three supercomputers to MacGyver an alternate system to control the gate on Earth. The SGC now uses an elaborate dialing computer to control the stargate and to initiate additional security protocols.

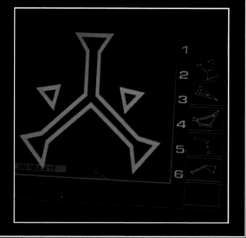

A dialing computer inputs coordinates.

AUTOMATIC CORRELATIVE UPDATE

In order to compensate for stellar drift, the stargate network undergoes periodic correlative updates in which the gates dial each other and automatically transmit new coordinates that apply to each gate address.

Memory crystals within the DHD are periodically updated.

MANUAL DIAL

It is possible to dial the stargate manually by using an external power source and spinning the inside wheel by hand. SG-1 has dialed the gate manually in emergency situations when no DHD was available, relying on such power sources as lightning, cold fusion, or two truck batteries.

Gate activation using cold fusion and manual dial

An iris was installed for additional security.

IRIS

A retractable iris of a trinium-titanium alloy is less than 3 microns from the event horizon and prevents unauthorized entry.

GDO

The GDO, or "Garage Door Opener," is the remote transmitter worn by each SG member while off-world.

SAFETY PROTOCOLS

When connected to a DHD, the stargate uses up to 400 safety protocols during a dialing sequence. A stargate cannot engage when it is buried, although it can activate when under water and when a closed iris is placed at least 3 microns from the event horizon, allowing a wormhole to form. A wormhole will not connect to a stargate that is already active, and similarly, an incoming wormhole prevents a gate from dialing out. A wormhole will remain active as long as any kind of matter or wave energy is passing through the event horizon, up to a maximum of 38 minutes under normal circumstances.

Frequency dampeners and modifications have corrected early problems with vibration, freezing temperatures, and rough transit.

IDC

The GDO transmitter sends an identification code, or IDC, to signal the SGC to open the iris for incoming travelers.

PALM SCANNER

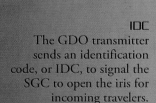

Following the Reetou incident, a palm scanner was installed to control the iris and wormhole activation and to prevent security breaches.

AVENGER

Dr. Jay Felger created Avenger 2.0, a computer virus named for a comic book hero, designed to scramble a DHD's coordinates and render a target gate useless to the Goa'uld. Within hours the entire stargate network shut down.

Brig. General Jack O'Neill

Weapons expert and skilled sharpshooter

BRIGADIER GENERAL JACK O'NEILL has helped to shape the SGC, and Earth owes a great deal to his courage and integrity. His Special Forces training has included covert operations and infiltration, special weapons and tactics, and survival skills, and he is a decorated parachutist and experienced pilot. As a career officer, he has spent many years in the service of his country, much of that time in covert Black Ops, and most of his work during these years has been classified.

Decorated parachutist and outstanding pilot

SG-1 patch

U.S. Air Force patch

Bugaboo glacier glasses

Earth patch

Jack O'Neill, ID #799 36 6412, Blood type B negative

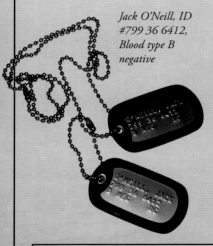

EXCEPTIONAL LEADER

O'Neill has earned a reputation for courage and heroism. A private person, he tends to use humor and sarcasm as a means of deflecting tension, and to exhibit a certain denseness that belies his true intelligence. Despite a tendency for irreverence and more than a few marks of insubordination on his record, he is highly respected as an exceptional military strategist and a decisive leader.

Charlie O'Neill

Sara O'Neill

FAMILY

O'Neill had been happily married to Sara, and together they had a son, Charlie. Despite O'Neill's military background, he never allowed his son to play with guns, but two weeks after a disagreement about a water pistol, young Charlie accidentally shot and killed himself with his father's handgun. O'Neill never forgave himself. He grew estranged from his wife, left the military, and withdrew from the world.

Beretta 92R pistol

CAREER

In 1982, Captain O'Neill and Captain Kawalsky served under Colonel John Michaels during Operation East Fly, a failed mission to retrieve a Russian agent from East Germany. In Iraq, O'Neill served with Frank Cromwell. When their mission was exposed, O'Neill was injured, and Cromwell, believing him to be dead, made the decision to save the rest of the team. O'Neill was left behind and spent four months in an Iraqi prison, which strengthened his fierce determination that no member of his team should ever be left behind.

Frank Cromwell

Charles Kawalsky

INTERESTS

O'Neill's eclectic interests range from astronomy to opera to pottery. An avid sports enthusiast, he enjoys hockey, baseball, football, golf, and curling, and his taste in television includes "The Simpsons," for which he owns the entire collection on VHS. He loves spending time outdoors, and for relaxation he enjoys nothing more than fishing at his cabin in northern Minnesota, 20 miles from the nearest town. Despite his insistence that he has never actually caught a fish, he maintains that the act of fishing is more important than the fish themselves.

MILITARY DECORATIONS

O'Neill is a distinguished and highly decorated officer with numerous medals for exemplary courage and heroism. Although he does not wear pilot's wings, he has flown several alien/hybrid craft including the F-302, for which he is the most qualified pilot on the planet.

Distinguished military officer

Master Parachutist badge, command level

Master Space/Missile badge, command level

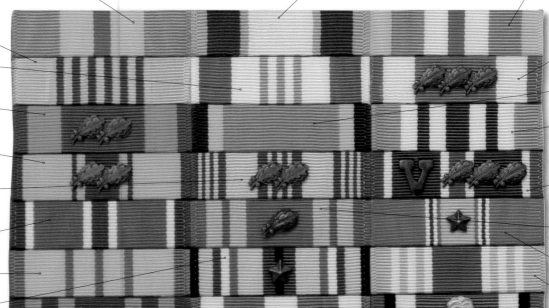

Defense Distinguished Service Medal

Air Force Distinguished Service Medal

Defense Superior Service Medal

Airman's Medal

Defense Meritorious Service Medal

Air Medal, 3rd Award

Air Force Commendation Medal, 3rd Award

Air Force Achievement Medal, 3rd Award

Air Force Organizational Excellence Award

Vietnam Service Medal

Southwest Asia Service Medal, 2nd Award

Meritorious Service Medal, 4th Award

Aerial Achievement Medal

Joint Service Commendation Medal

Air Force Outstanding Unit Award with Valor, 4th Award

Combat Readiness Medal, 2nd Award

National Defense Service Medal, 2nd Award

Air Force Overseas Ribbon—Short Tour

Air Force Longevity Service Award, 4th Award

Republic of Vietnam Campaign Medal

Kuwait Liberation Medal, Kingdom of Saudi Arabia, with Palm

Brig. General Jack O'Neill

W HEN THE STARGATE was first activated and a team was assembled for the first mission to Abydos, Colonel O'Neill, still distraught over the death of his son, accepted the assignment, believing it to be a suicide mission, but he returned from Abydos instead with renewed hope and quietly settled into retirement alone. In 1997, he was again recalled to active duty for the return mission to Abydos, and he took command of the newly formed flagship team, SG-1.

The knowledge of the Ancients was downloaded into O'Neill's mind.

ANCIENT REPOSITORY

On P3R-272, SG-1 first encountered an Ancient repository which downloaded the knowledge of the Ancients into O'Neill's mind. As the vast database slowly began to overwrite his brain, he began to unwillingly speak the Ancient language, to enter new stargate addresses into the SGC database, and to build an energy generator that allowed the stargate to dial the Asgard planet of Othala where he could seek help.

THE ASGARD

O'Neill has earned the respect of Earth's allies including the Asgard, Nox, and Tollans. Among the Asgard, O'Neill had become legendary due to the presence of the Ancient gene in his genetic makeup which enables him to interact with Ancient technology such as the Ancient repository. Thor's admiration for O'Neill's abilities led him to personally select O'Neill to represent Earth in the negotiations for the Protected Planets Treaty, and to name the Asgard's most advanced spaceship, the *O'Neill*, in his honor.

KANAN

When O'Neill reluctantly agreed to become a host to the Tok'ra, Kanan, the symbiote instead used O'Neill's body to return to Ba'al's highly fortified outpost. With no memory of what had brought him to the secret facility, O'Neill became Ba'al's prisoner and was repeatedly tortured to death, then revived in a sarcophagus. Weakened to the point of breaking, he withstood the ordeal only to protect Ba'al's slave whom Kanan had hoped to rescue.

The mutual respect between O'Neill and Thor has led to a firm alliance between Earth and the Asgard.

Ba'al

THE BATTLE FOR EARTH

O'Neill has never hesitated to put the fate of the planet before his own life. When the discovery of a second Ancient repository on P3X-439 gave SG-1 the opportunity to defeat Anubis, O'Neill made the decision to interface with the device once again, hoping to access the knowledge to save Earth before the technology would lead to his death. Even as his own identity began to slip away, O'Neill accessed the address of Praclarush Taonas, and activated the Ancient defense weapon in Antarctica, defeating Anubis and saving Earth from annihilation.

O'Neill activated the Ancient defense weapon in Antarctica.

VITAL STATISTICS

Born in Chicago and raised in Minnesota, O'Neill seldom speaks of his formative years. He rarely mentions his parents, and he has no known siblings, although he has referred fondly to his grandfather from northern Minnesota. Occasionally addressed as Jonathan, O'Neill is identified on his security ID as Colonel Jack O'Neill, born October 20, 1952.

Jack O'Neill's military ID

USAF

COL. O'NEILL, JACK

RANK
COLONEL

DATE OF BIRTH
20 /10 / 52

STATUS
ACTIVE

Following General Hammond's reassignment to Washington, O'Neill took command of the SGC.

FACT FILE

IN THE LINE OF DUTY

O'Neill has suffered nine broken bones, including skull fractures, three knee surgeries, internal injuries, hypothermia, anoxia, concussion, shrapnel, a dislocated shoulder, and exposure to muon radiation, Hathor's organism, nish'ta, the Blood of Sokar, the plants of Paradise, the mind control of Nem, the Keeper, Urgo, the memory stamp, the light, and the Ancient repository. He has been impaled by the orb, switched bodies with Daniel and Teal'c, possessed by Anubis, implanted by both Tok'ra and Goa'uld, infected by a histaminolytic virus, an Ancient virus, a nano-virus, and Ma'chello's inventions, cryogenically frozen, and duplicated by the Unity crystals, Harlan, the aliens of P3X-118, and Loki. He has been wounded by an arrow and by alien weapons, tortured by the Goa'uld torture device and tal'vak acid, attacked by energy beings, and given the abdominal pouch of a Jaffa. He has sustained two bullet wounds, three staff weapon wounds, five incidents of a ribbon device, and eleven shots by a zat'nik'tel, and he has been killed by Apophis, by laser fire in a future reality, and was repeatedly tortured to death and revived in a sarcophagus at the hands of Ba'al.

BRIGADIER GENERAL

Following the defeat of Anubis, O'Neill was promoted from colonel to brigadier general and offered the command of the SGC. He accepted the assignment, and although the transition to an administrative role at first caused him to question his ability to fill Hammond's shoes and led him to consider resignation, his somewhat unorthodox leadership style has served him well, and he has proven himself to be an exceptional general.

Dr. Daniel Jackson

D ANIEL JACKSON EMBODIES the passion of SG-1, and brings to his team not only his skills as an exceptional linguist and archaeologist, but also a curiosity and a sense of wonder and discovery. Daniel was born on July 8, 1965, the son of archaeologists Dr. Melburn and Claire Jackson. He has no known siblings, and when he was only 8 years old, his parents were crushed to death when a temple exhibit collapsed in a freak accident at the New York Museum of Art.

Daniel most often wears glasses.

FAMILY TIES

Daniel's grandfather, Nicholas Ballard, was also a renowned archaeologist, known for his discovery of the crystal skull of Belize two years before. Ballard chose not to adopt his young grandson, and pursued his career instead. Daniel was raised by foster parents, and chose archaeology as his own career as well.

Daniel with his grandfather, Nicholas Ballard

Earth patch

PASSIONATE EXPLORER

Daniel is highly respected by his teammates. As a scientist, he shares Carter's passion for exploration and thirst for knowledge, and he has come to admire Teal'c's quiet strength and sense of purpose. O'Neill and Daniel share a mutual respect and admiration strengthened by the contrast in their personalities, O'Neill's decisive leadership skills balanced by Daniel's tendency to approach issues through diplomacy and negotiation.

MEMORIAL SERVICE

SG-1 was led to believe that Daniel had died on Oannes, and at his memorial service, O'Neill voiced his admiration for his teammate. "Daniel Jackson made this place happen. As a member of SG-1, he was our voice, our conscience. He was a very courageous man. He was a good man. For those of us lucky enough to have known him, he was also a friend."

EDUCATION

Daniel earned his Ph.D. in archaeology, his particular area of expertise being ancient cultures and languages. He studied under Dr. David Jordan in Chicago, and his colleagues while at university included Steven Rayner, who grew resentful of his abilities, Robert Rothman, who was his research assistant as he prepared his dissertation, and Sarah Gardner, with whom he had been romantically involved until his obsession with his research destroyed their relationship. At first highly respected in the field of archaeology, Daniel was eventually laughed out of academia for his controversial theories of alien involvement in ancient cultures, and for his hypotheses that Egyptian civilization is thousands of years older than suspected and that the great pyramids were built as landing sites for alien ships.

David Jordan

Robert Rothman

Sarah Gardner

Steven Rayner

LINGUIST AND DIPLOMAT

Daniel's facility with languages is extraordinary, and he claims to speak 23 different languages including German, Russian, Spanish, Latin, Phoenician, Babylonian, Mayan, and ancient Egyptian. He also has the ability to interpret hieroglyphics, cuneiform, and Nordic runes, and his natural gift for languages has allowed him to acquire a fluency in several alien languages including Abydonian, Goa'uld, Unas, and Ancient. As an archaeologist, Daniel has provided invaluable insight into the cultures SG-1 has encountered, and he has exhibited an exceptional ability as a diplomat, having helped to broker numerous important negotiations both on Earth and with alien cultures.

IN THE LINE OF DUTY

Daniel has frequently endured physical trauma including wounds and torture from alien weapons, multiple injuries from Reese, Vala, Soren's revolution, and a rock slide, and he has been felled by appendicitis. He has come under the influence of Hathor's organism, nish'ta, the Blood of Sokar, and the mind control of Nem, the Keeper, Urgo, Osiris, the memory stamp, the light, Shifu's dream, and Replicator Carter. He has switched bodies with O'Neill and Ma'chello, been possessed by the entity of Anubis, and has served as a "lifeboat" for a dozen personalities. He has been infected by a histaminolytic virus and Ma'chello's inventions, cryogenically frozen, duplicated by Harlan and by the aliens of P3X-118, and transported to a dimension of invisibility. He sustained two bullet wounds, two staff weapon wounds, and nine shots by a zat'nik'tel. Seven times he has faced the ribbon device, and he has endured the addictive effects of the sarcophagus. Four times he has died, having been killed by Apophis on the Nox world, by laser fire in a future reality, by radiation poisoning on Kelowna, and a stab wound to the heart at the hands of Replicator Carter.

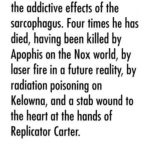

INTERESTS

Daniel's interests focus on the area of academics, and much of his free time is spent in intellectual pursuits, although he has been known to take advantage of the gym facilities at the SGC. He has a passion for reading, and even his taste in television tends toward the History Channel. He easily uses the computer as a research tool but is most at home surrounded by books or conducting archaeological research in the field. Daniel owns a piano and keeps a tank of tropical fish, and he is known as an avid coffee drinker.

Archaeological dig on P3X-888

Dr. Daniel Jackson

O N ABYDOS, DANIEL DISCOVERED a map room near the pyramid and an ancient cartouche that held the key to the known stargate addresses. His theory that the stargate could dial many planets beyond Abydos was later confirmed, and calculations to adjust for stellar drift made travel to other worlds possible. When Apophis arrived through the Abydos gate and captured Sha're and Skaara, Daniel left his adopted home and returned to Earth to become a member of SG-1 and join the battle against the Goa'uld.

Daniel adopted the sandy, desert planet of Abydos as his home.

CATHERINE LANGFORD
At the lowest point of his career, Daniel was recruited by Catherine Langford to work on the stargate project. It was Daniel who solved the mysteries of the gate, and the Stargate Program was born.

Catherine Langford

SHA'RE
Daniel was reunited with Sha're on Abydos, but Amaunet, the Goa'uld who possessed her, reemerged after she gave birth to the child of Apophis. A year later SG-1 encountered Amaunet on P8X-873, and as she held Daniel in the grip of her ribbon device, Sha're communicated through the device her message of forgiveness and concern for her child. To save Daniel's life, Teal'c was forced to kill Amaunet, taking Sha're's life as well.

Amaunet and Daniel

ABYDOS
Daniel participated in the first mission to Abydos under Colonel O'Neill, and he chose to remain behind on the planet, taking Sha're, a native of Abydos, as his wife after she had been offered to him as a gift and the two had fallen in love. Despite the devastating loss of Sha're to the Goa'uld, Daniel found the capacity to redirect his life.

The death of Sha're

ASCENSION

On a mission to Kelowna, SG-1 encountered a civilization developing a naquadria weapon of mass destruction. A laboratory accident threatened to destroy the planet, and Daniel risked his life to disarm the device, exposing himself to lethal radiation. As his body succumbed to radiation poisoning, Oma Desala helped to guide him toward enlightenment, and Daniel chose ascension, taking on the non-corporeal form of the Others, to continue his journey on a higher plane of existence.

Oma Desala

Daniel urged O'Neill to let him go, and to allow him to ascend.

FALLEN

As an ascended being, Daniel had the power to accomplish great tasks, but was not permitted to intervene in human affairs. Angered by what he perceived to be injustice, he chose to return to human form, to continue to fight for humanity, but at the cost of losing all that he had learned as an ascended being. In a brilliant flash of light on the planet Vis Uban, Daniel was returned to human form, naked, alone, and with no memory of his past. There he was reunited with SG-1 and eventually regained his memory and his place on the team.

A HIGHER PLANE

When Daniel was captured and killed by Replicator Carter, he was once again offered the choice between death and ascension. On another plane of existence, Daniel encountered both Oma Desala and Anubis, and came to realize what he had learned before, that the rules of noninterference were Oma's punishment for unknowingly helping Anubis to ascend. This time, however, Oma Desala made the choice to take action, and as she confronted Anubis in eternal struggle, Daniel was returned once again to human form.

Replicator Carter sought the knowledge of the Ancients in Daniel's mind.

Oma Desala appeared as a waitress in a cosmic diner between planes of existence.

FACT FILE

SHIFU

Shifu, the child of Sha're by Apophis, hoped to show Daniel the evil of absolute power. Through a dream, he taught that the true nature of a man is determined in the battle between his conscious mind and the desires of his subconscious, and that in the struggle against evil, "The only way to win is to deny it battle."

Shifu

THE DANIEL JACKSON

Following the destruction of the *Biliskner* and the Asgard prototype ship, the *O'Neill*, a new class of Asgard motherships was developed. Thor took command of a ship from this new fleet, and in a gesture of respect for his Earth allies, named it the *Daniel Jackson*.

Lt. Col. Samantha Carter

SAMANTHA CARTER IS A BRILLIANT SCIENTIST and military officer. Her father, Jacob Carter, had been a general in the U.S. Air Force. Her mother had died tragically in an auto accident when Carter was a teenager, and her relationship with her father and her brother Mark became strained after the devastating loss. Ever since she was a little girl, Carter had wanted to become an astronaut, but she redirected her energies after the suspension of the shuttle program following the Challenger disaster, and she followed her father into a career in the Air Force.

Samantha Carter, ID #456 731 479, Blood type A positive

SGC Vest

Radio

P-90 Submachine Gun

Young Samantha Carter

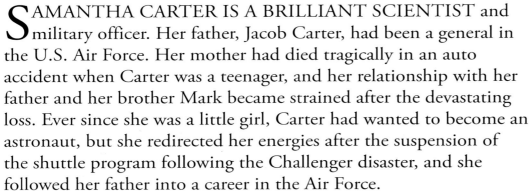

Jacob Carter

TRAINING

Carter is an outstanding military officer. She logged over 100 hours in enemy airspace during the Gulf War and has completed simulated bombing runs in an F-16. Although she does not wear pilot's wings, she has had training as a pilot, and has flown both first seat and second seat in alien/ hybrid craft such as the F-302. She has reached level three advanced in hand-to-hand combat training.

Experienced pilot

Combat Bracelet

Zat'nik'tel

Taking first seat in the F-302

Suunto Black Vector Watch

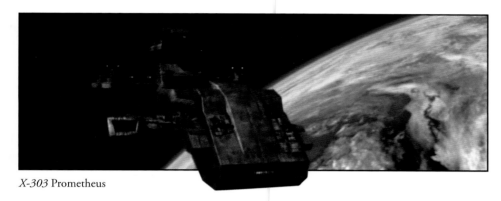

SCIENTIFIC CONTRIBUTIONS

Carter's knowledge of science and technology has been a tremendous asset to the Stargate Program. Her extensive familiarity with alien technology and design has enabled her to repair, reverse engineer, and interface with many kinds of alien devices. She has been actively involved in the design and construction of the hybrid technology used in the development of the X-301, X-302, and X-303 series of human-built spacecraft.

X-302

X-303 Prometheus

FACT FILE

ACCOMPLISHMENTS

Carter is considered by many to be Earth's foremost expert on the stargate. Her early research at the Pentagon helped to lay the foundation of Earth's current understanding of wormhole physics.

As a brilliant mathematician and an expert in computer systems, Carter is often called upon to write programs or to work with encryption or data retrieval and analysis.

Carter has designed and modified a number of pieces of technology including hybrid spacecraft and a particle beam accelerator. Her modification of a design from the planet Orban led to the development of a viable naquadah generator which has become an invaluable power source.

Carter's knowledge of astrophysics has even allowed her to accomplish the formidable task of creating an artificial supernova to blow up a sun.

PROMOTIONS

After two years of exemplary service with the SGC, Captain Carter was promoted to the rank of major, and on several missions she was given temporary command of the SG-1 unit in the absence of Colonel O'Neill. Five years after achieving the rank of major, she was promoted to the rank of lieutenant colonel, and following O'Neill's promotion to general, Carter became the commanding officer of SG-1.

Promotion to Major Carter

EDUCATION

Carter has devoted her life to her work. She followed in her father's footsteps and entered the US Air Force Academy where she studied and trained under General Kerrigan and Professor Monroe, and she proved to have a brilliant scientific and mathematical mind. She earned her Ph.D. in theoretical astrophysics, and transferred to the Pentagon in Washington, DC. There she spent a year studying nano-technology, she worked with Dr. Timothy Harlow in the field of genetics, and she broke new ground with her research into wormhole physics.

Carter earned a Ph.D. in theoretical astrophysics.

Carter is a decorated military officer.

MILITARY DECORATIONS

Carter's brilliant military career has brought her many recognitions and honors. She received a special commendation after her actions prevented Hathor from acquiring control of the SGC, and she has been recognized numerous times for distinguished courage and heroism.

Space/Missile Badge, senior level

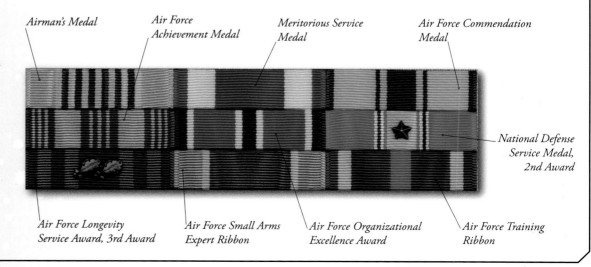

Airman's Medal | *Air Force Achievement Medal* | *Meritorious Service Medal* | *Air Force Commendation Medal* | *National Defense Service Medal, 2nd Award*

Air Force Longevity Service Award, 3rd Award | *Air Force Small Arms Expert Ribbon* | *Air Force Organizational Excellence Award* | *Air Force Training Ribbon*

Lt. Col. Samantha Carter

CARTER HELPED TO PIONEER the field of wormhole physics. At the Pentagon she studied gate technology and worked to develop the Stargate Program two years before the gate was activated for the first Abydos mission. Following the arrival of Apophis through the Earth stargate, a team was assembled for a military response. As an expert on the stargate, Carter was transferred from the Pentagon to Cheyenne Mountain to participate in the second mission to Abydos, and at the rank of captain, she became a member of SG-1 under Colonel O'Neill.

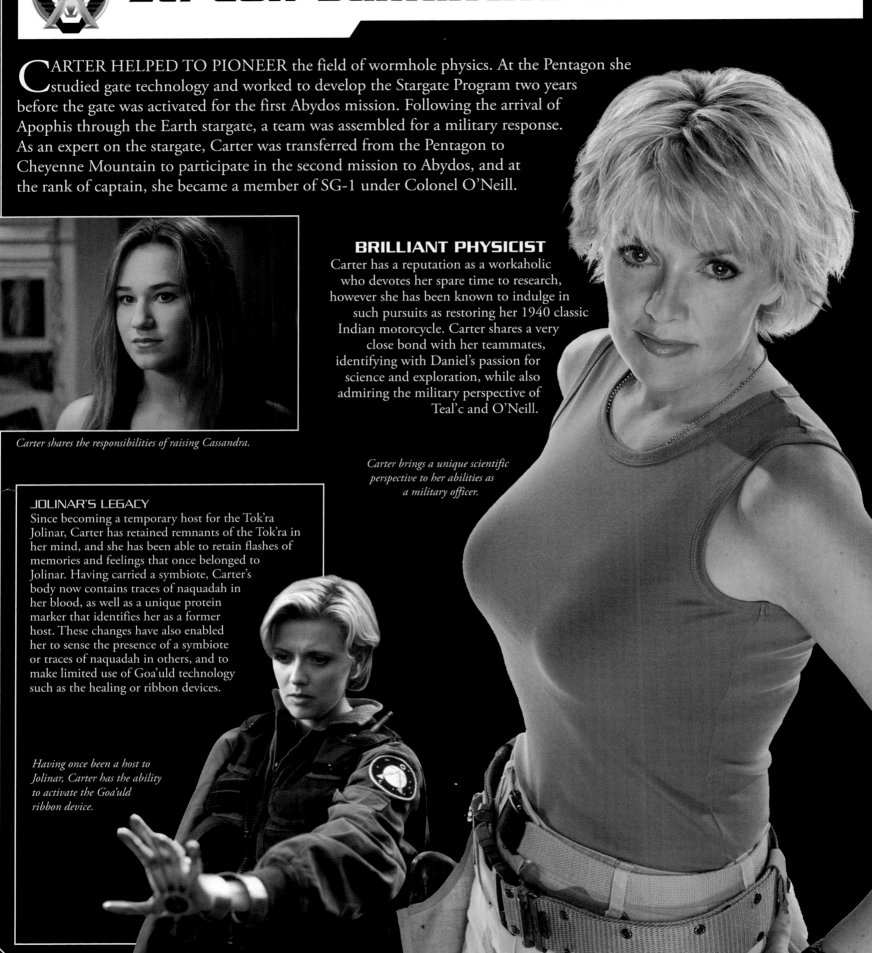

Carter shares the responsibilities of raising Cassandra.

BRILLIANT PHYSICIST

Carter has a reputation as a workaholic who devotes her spare time to research, however she has been known to indulge in such pursuits as restoring her 1940 classic Indian motorcycle. Carter shares a very close bond with her teammates, identifying with Daniel's passion for science and exploration, while also admiring the military perspective of Teal'c and O'Neill.

Carter brings a unique scientific perspective to her abilities as a military officer.

JOLINAR'S LEGACY

Since becoming a temporary host for the Tok'ra Jolinar, Carter has retained remnants of the Tok'ra in her mind, and she has been able to retain flashes of memories and feelings that once belonged to Jolinar. Having carried a symbiote, Carter's body now contains traces of naquadah in her blood, as well as a unique protein marker that identifies her as a former host. These changes have also enabled her to sense the presence of a symbiote or traces of naquadah in others, and to make limited use of Goa'uld technology such as the healing or ribbon devices.

Having once been a host to Jolinar, Carter has the ability to activate the Goa'uld ribbon device.

JACOB CARTER

Carter was reunited with both her father and the Tok'ra when Jacob Carter was dying of cancer and volunteered to become a host to the Tok'ra symbiote Selmak. Jacob became a liaison between the SGC and the Tok'ra, and with many of the past wounds between them healed, the relationship between Carter and her father became closer than it had ever been.

RELATIONSHIPS

Carter was briefly engaged to Jonas Hanson before joining the SGC, and several men encountered on alien worlds have developed an attraction to her, including Narim of the Tollan, Martouf of the Tok'ra, and Orlin, an ascended being. Carter has also shared a special bond with O'Neill, a personal relationship which has remained professional.

Martouf of the Tok'ra

Narim of the Tollan

PETE SHANAHAN

Carter's relationship with Pete Shanahan, a cop from Denver, developed into a romance, and about a year after they met, Carter accepted Pete's proposal of marriage. As their wedding date approached, however, Carter began to question her decision. At the same time she faced emotional turmoil as her father confessed that he was dying and urged her to follow her heart. Carter was with Jacob as he peacefully passed away, but following her father's death, she met with Pete and gently broke off their engagement.

Carter was briefly engaged to Pete Shanahan.

FACT FILE

IN THE LINE OF DUTY

Carter has sustained injuries from alien weapons and physical trauma, a massive concussion, four lacerations, electrical burns, and exposure to muon radiation. She has come under the influence of nish'ta, the Blood of Sokar, the mind control of Nem, the Keeper, Urgo, the memory stamp, the light, Fifth, and her Replicator double. She was taken as a host by Jolinar, an immature symbiote, and the entity of Anubis, infected by a histaminolytic virus and an Ancient virus, cryogenically frozen, and duplicated by Harlan and Fifth. She has been subjected to Nirrti's DNA resequencer, the Ashrak's harakash, five exposures to a ribbon device, and nine shots from a zat'nik'tel. She was killed by Apophis on the Nox world and by laser fire in a future reality, and when she was taken as a host by the Entity, her consciousness was removed as her body was killed.

JOLINAR

On a mission to Nasya during her second year of service with SG-1, Carter was taken as a host by Jolinar of Malkshur, a Tok'ra symbiote who was fleeing assassination by the Ashrak and leapt from a dying host into Carter to hide. Unable to escape the Ashrak, however, Jolinar was severely tortured, and she made the choice to sacrifice her life in order to save Carter's. Carter still retains some of Jolinar's memories, knowledge, and abilities, and those memories led SG-1 to first encounter the Tok'ra on P34-353J.

Jolinar attempted to flee through the stargate but was detained on Earth and eventually sacrificed her life to save Carter's.

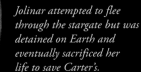

Teal'c

First Prime of Apophis

TEAL'C HAS PROVEN himself to be a warrior of outstanding integrity. As a Jaffa, Teal'c's life has been extended by the symbiotes he has carried since childhood. Born over 100 years ago, Teal'c, whose name means "strength," is the son of Ronac, once the First Prime of Cronus. For failure in battle against impossible odds, Ronac was killed by Cronus, and young Teal'c and his mother fled to Chulak. Driven by vengeance, Teal'c vowed to one day become the First Prime of Apophis.

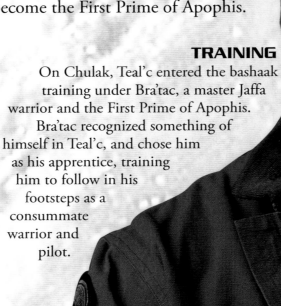

Serpent tattoo of Apophis's Jaffa

TRAINING

On Chulak, Teal'c entered the bashaak training under Bra'tac, a master Jaffa warrior and the First Prime of Apophis. Bra'tac recognized something of himself in Teal'c, and chose him as his apprentice, training him to follow in his footsteps as a consummate warrior and pilot.

BRA'TAC

Bra'tac taught Teal'c that the Goa'uld were false gods, but despite his doubts, Teal'c entered Apophis's personal guard, eventually succeeding Bra'tac as Apophis's First Prime.

Retractable Helmet

Shoulder patch designating SG-1

Reinforced Armor

Chain Mail

Teal'c wearing the Serpent Guard armor of a Jaffa warrior.

FIRST PRIME OF APOPHIS

Wearing the gold forehead tattoo of his rank as First Prime, Teal'c served Apophis for many years, witnessing and committing countless atrocities, including the harvesting of human hosts for the Goa'uld. As his doubts grew, Teal'c's hatred for the Goa'uld intensified, and he began to strengthen his dedication to the cause of freedom for all Jaffa from the slavery of the Goa'uld.

Apophis

ISHTA

Teal'c's struggle against the Goa'uld brought him to the world of the Hak'tyl where he met Ishta, with whom he has shared a strong mutual attraction despite their different views. Rya'c, too, found companionship among the Hak'tyl, and he married Kar'yn, one of Ishta's followers, a union of which Teal'c did not initially approve, believing his son was too young to know love, but which he has come to openly accept.

Ishta of the Hak'tyl

FAMILY

When Teal'c joined the Tauri, he left behind a family on Chulak, and his wife, Drey'auc, and son, Rya'c, became outcasts following his betrayal. Teal'c returned to Chulak, hoping to prevent the prim'ta of his son, but Rya'c was dying, and to save his life, Teal'c gave him his own symbiote, taking a new larva for himself. When Apophis kidnapped Rya'c, Teal'c returned once more to rescue his family and sent them to live in the Land of Light.

Shoulder patch designating Earth

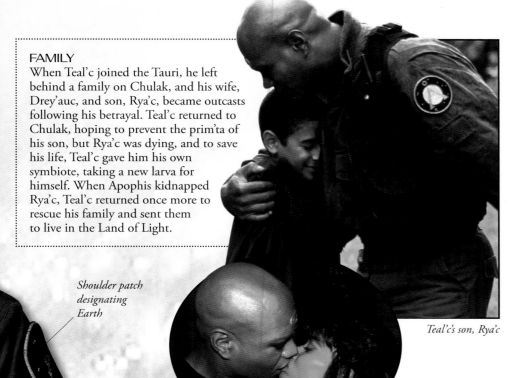

Teal'c's son, Rya'c

STOIC WARRIOR

Teal'c's quiet strength conceals a proud and passionate character. Dignified and intensely loyal, he exhibits both a fierce determination and a gentle compassion. His stoic demeanor has softened during his years on Earth, allowing subtle glimpses of sadness and humor. He feels tremendous respect for Daniel and Carter, and in O'Neill he sees a fellow warrior, a leader worthy of his unquestioning loyalty, with whom he shares an understanding that requires few words.

Teal'c's wife, Drey'auc

INTERESTS

Since coming to Earth, Teal'c has discovered something of the ways of the Tauri. He has continued to practice his martial arts while also discovering an interest in weight training, boxing, golf, and ping pong. He has developed a taste for tabloid journalism, vibrating beds, jello wrestling, doughnuts, and science fiction movies, especially "Star Wars," which he claims to have seen nine times. He learned to drive from Daniel in 1969, and from O'Neill he learned the fine art of juggling, although he has not acquired O'Neill's interest in fishing.

FACT FILE

"MURRAY"

Although he had once insisted that his head must be shaved, after seven years on Earth Teal'c allowed his hair to grow. When venturing out in public on Earth, he often indulges in his taste for 70's fashion and has an impressive collection of hats to cover his tattoo. He occasionally adopts the nickname "Murray," given to him by O'Neill.

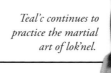

Teal'c continues to practice the martial art of lok'nel.

Teal'c

I T WAS TEAL'C WHO SELECTED Daniel's wife, Sha're, to become the host to Amaunet, but when he encountered SG-1 in the prison on Chulak, Teal'c recognized in Jack O'Neill a warrior who had tasted freedom. In that moment, he turned against his god and joined the Tauri. Although O'Neill and Teal'c formed an instant bond of trust, Teal'c earned the trust of others on Earth and at the Pentagon more slowly. However, after proving his loyalty, Teal'c joined SG-1 and the fight against the Goa'uld.

Teal'c betrayed his god and joined SG-1.

RITE OF M'AL SHARRAN

Declared the "Shol'va," the traitor, when he joined the Tauri, Teal'c became the target of Apophis's revenge. When he was captured and killed on Vorash, then revived in the sarcophagus, Teal'c was led to believe that he was once again Apophis's First Prime. However, his soul was restored by Bra'tac, who forced him to endure the Rite of M'al Sharran, as his symbiote was removed and he was taken to the very threshold of death to rediscover his true path and return to SG-1.

Teal'c was killed on Vorash.

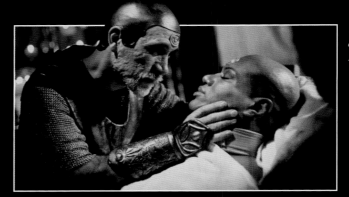

Taken to the brink of death, few survive the Rite of M'al Sharran.

REBEL JAFFA

Teal'c dedicated himself to the SGC and the fight against the Goa'uld, but his dream continued to be the liberation of his people, and he gave his loyalty to Bra'tac and the growing movement of the Rebel Jaffa. Teal'c also faced a difficult reunion with his son. Rya'c had grown strong in the ways of the Jaffa under the teachings of Master Bra'tac, but he had also grown resentful of his father's decision to abandon his family. After an uneasy reconciliation, Rya'c joined his father's cause.

Teal'c's loyalties are to the SGC and to freedom for all Jaffa.

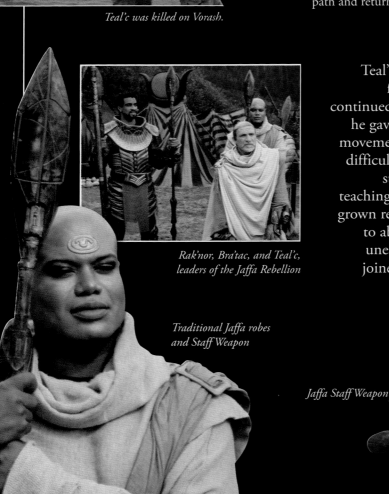

Rak'nor, Bra'tac, and Teal'c, leaders of the Jaffa Rebellion

Traditional Jaffa robes and Staff Weapon

Jaffa Staff Weapon

Following the Ambush of Kresh'taa, regular doses of tretonin have allowed Teal'c to live without the reliance on a symbiote.

AMBUSH OF KRESH'TAA

When a summit of Rebel Jaffa leaders was ambushed, over one hundred Rebel warriors were slaughtered and only Teal'c and Bra'tac were left alive, sharing the healing powers of Teal'c's symbiote between them for three days before they were rescued. During that time, Teal'c slipped in and out of consciousness, and in disjointed images he imagined himself as "T," a human living on Earth. Throughout the ordeal he was sustained by Daniel, who spoke to him from his ascended form through Teal'c's dreams.

The Ambush of Kresh'taa

Teal'c imagines himself as human

Daniel spoke through Teal'c's dreams.

DAKARA

As the Rebel cause faced a critical turn, it was Teal'c who proposed capturing the holy site at Dakara. With the defeat of the Replicators and Anubis, the conquest of Dakara succeeded, and on that holy ground the Rebel Jaffa prepared to build a great city that would be the heart of the new Jaffa homeworld. With their victory, Tolok bestowed upon Teal'c and Bra'tac the highest honor a Jaffa can know, for their enduring courage and vision that had brought freedom from the Goa'uld. Henceforth, Teal'c shall be known as Blood Kin to all Jaffa.

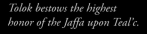
Tolok bestows the highest honor of the Jaffa upon Teal'c.

SHAN'AUC

Teal'c's poignant reunion with Shan'auc, a temple priestess from his past, rekindled a romance and offered a means of defeating the Goa'uld until the dream was abruptly shattered by Shan'auc's death at the hands of Tanith, the symbiote she had carried. Driven by his determination to avenge her death, Teal'c continued to work tirelessly to bring other Jaffa to the Rebel cause.

FACT FILE

IN THE LINE OF DUTY

Teal'c has been wounded by alien weapons, a knife, shrapnel, and electrical burns. He has sustained massive internal injuries and head trauma, and endured the Rite of M'al Sharran and the Ambush of Kresh'taa. He has come under the influence of the mind control technology of Nem, the Keeper, Urgo, and the memory stamp, has switched bodies with O'Neill and Ma'chello, been possessed by alien water beings, and duplicated by Harlan. He has been blinded, subjected to the effects of Thor's Hammer and Ma'chello's inventions, trapped within the stargate matrix, and has suffered a cardiac arrest and undergone a metamorphosis. He has endured torture from the Goa'uld torture device, ribbon device, and whipping, and sustained four bullet wounds, four staff weapon wounds, and four shots from a zat'nik'tel. Brought to the brink of death several times, he has also drowned, been killed by laser fire in a future reality, and killed by a staff weapon wound, only to be revived and brainwashed in a sarcophagus.

HOME

After seven years, Teal'c was permitted an apartment off base on the condition that he maintain a low profile. He explained to neighbors that his friend, Dr. Jackson, an archaeologist, had hired him to come from Mozambique, and that his tattoo was a tribal mark from his homeland. His excursion off base was short-lived, however. He insisted on intervening in the prevention of neighborhood crime, and surveillance by the Trust led to blackmail and false charges of kidnapping and murder. Despite being cleared in the investigation, Teal'c remained a target of the Trust, and chose to return to his quarters on the base.

Jaffa chic with an East African flair

Jonas Quinn

JONAS QUINN HAD BEEN THE SPECIAL ADVISOR to the High Minister of Kelowna. With a brilliant and educated mind, Jonas was considered a man of unique talents on his world, and he earned several degrees at Kelowna's most honored educational institution. He studied with Dr. Kieran, a professor and researcher at the Academy of Science, and was recruited by his friend and mentor into the Naquadria Project. They had been working together for six years when SG-1 first arrived on Kelowna, and Jonas enthusiastically welcomed the visitors to his world.

NAQUADRIA PROJECT
Jonas was present when tragedy struck, and he witnessed the lab accident which exposed Daniel to lethal radiation. He reported the incident to his superiors, but was ashamed by his government's attempt to conceal the truth. At the risk of being considered a traitor by his people, Jonas brought a sample of naquadria to the SGC.

Jonas shared naquadria with Earth in the hope of developing defensive technologies.

LIFE ON EARTH
Unable to return to his homeworld, Jonas settled in at the SGC where he memorized most of the mission reports and journals in the base archive and mastered several new languages including Ancient. What Jonas longed for, however, was the opportunity to join the exploration of the galaxy, to fight the Goa'uld, and to find a way to help make up for the loss of Daniel. After three months at the SGC, Jonas earned O'Neill's recommendation as an official member of SG-1.

Jonas graduated from an in'tar to a P-90

Jonas learns and retains information more quickly than the average human.

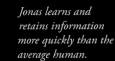

Jonas recorded detailed journals and notebooks.

Nirrti's DNA resequencer caused the development of a unique brain tumor.

DR. KIERAN

When a Kelownan delegation arrived seeking military aid from Earth, First Minister Valis offered Jonas a full pardon to return home to his former position, but Jonas chose to remain with SG-1. The delegation also presented a bittersweet reunion with Dr. Kieran when it became apparent that the increasingly erratic behavior of Jonas's friend was due to a unique form of brain damage caused by prolonged exposure to naquadria radiation.

DNA RESEQUENCER

SG-1 was captured by Nirrti on P3X-367 and subjected to her DNA resequencer, a device which detected Jonas's advanced genetic makeup. It caused the development, some weeks later, of an unusual tumor in Jonas's brain, a life threatening nonmalignant astrocytoma that caused headaches, seizures, and limited precognitive abilities. Emergency surgery to remove the tumor was successful, and Jonas's precognitive flashes vanished.

Exposure to naquadria produces symptoms of schizophrenia and paranoia, but tests on Jonas for the disorder were negative.

FACT FILE

IN THE LINE OF DUTY

During his tenure with SG-1, Jonas received several injuries in the line of duty. He was shot twice by a zat'nik'tel and received a staff weapon wound to the shoulder. He was infected by an Ancient virus and was the first to interact with the device from P9X-391 that made inter-dimensional beings visible. His mind was invaded by the human-form Replicators and by Anubis, who used a mind probe to access his knowledge, and he was subjected to Nirrti's DNA resequencer which subsequently caused the growth of a brain tumor that was successfully removed through surgery.

Jonas was shot by a zat'nik'tel on P2X-005.

HOMECOMING

As a prisoner of Anubis, Jonas was subjected to a mind probe through which Anubis learned of the naquadria native to his planet. Jonas's role in helping to defeat Anubis at Kelowna served to redeem him in the eyes of his countrymen, and the quarreling nations agreed to participate in a joint ruling council on the condition that Jonas serve as the Kelownan representative.

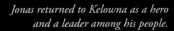
Jonas returned to Kelowna as a hero and a leader among his people.

FALLOUT

A crisis on Kelowna brought Jonas back to the SGC. With the cooperation of SG-1 and his research partner, Kianna Cyr, Jonas helped to pilot a deep underground excavation vehicle deep below Kelowna's surface to halt an advancing vein of unstable naquadria that threatened to obliterate his world.

Kianna had been taken as a host by a Goa'uld in Ba'al's service.

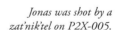
Jonas and Kianna had also shared a brief mutual attraction.

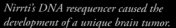

General George Hammond

EORGE HAMMOND WAS RAISED in Texas and began his military career at a young age. In 1969, as a young Air Force lieutenant, he had been assigned to the top secret missile silo at Cheyenne Mountain under Major Thornbird. There he had been ordered to escort four suspected Soviet spies for interrogation. In the vest pocket of one of them, he found a note with his name on it, written in his own handwriting. The note said "Help them." Without realizing it, he had met SG-1, and his future. Trusting the note, he helped SG-1 to escape, and in doing so he fulfilled his own destiny.

Hammond's own note to the past would return SG-1 home.

CAREER

Major General Hammond's career of 30 years had been a successful one. When he replaced General West as the commanding officer of the underground facility at Cheyenne Mountain, the stargate was inactive and his position was meant to be an easy duty on his way to a quiet retirement only one month away. Widowed four years earlier, with two young granddaughters, he was looking forward to writing his memoirs. He never suspected that Stargate Command would become the first line of defense for planet Earth.

STARGATE COMMAND

When Apophis stepped through the Earth stargate, the Stargate Program was initiated under Hammond's command. As the commanding officer of the SGC, Hammond answered directly to the Chief of Staff of the Air Force and the President of the United States, and he directed the action from Cheyenne Mountain beneath NORAD. Despite his cooperative relationship with the President, Hammond has had his critics within the NID, who threatened consequences against his family in an attempt to pressure him into stepping down. Hammond temporarily resigned until O'Neill restored his command by gathering evidence against the NID.

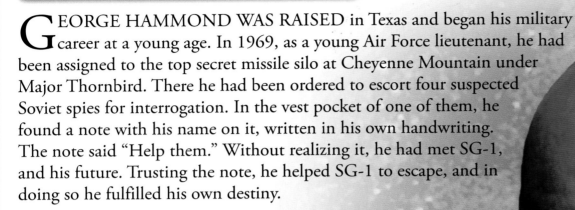

Command Pilot Badge, command level

Master Space/ Missile Badge, command level

General Hammond, commanding officer of the SGC.

Hammond and Daniel aboard the Prometheus

REASSIGNMENT

Newly elected President Hayes made the political decision to temporarily suspend SGC operations, and Dr. Elizabeth Weir was placed in charge of the facility. General Hammond was summoned to Washington, and although he felt the time had come to reconsider his long overdue retirement, Anubis's attack on Earth made his expertise all the more crucial. President Hayes ordered the launch of *Prometheus* with Hammond at the helm, and under his command the entire Earth fleet engaged Anubis in battle above Antarctica, allowing SG-1 to complete their mission and activate the Ancient defense weapon that saved Earth.

General Hammond commanded the Prometheus *in Antarctica.*

HOMEWORLD SECURITY

Following the battle to save Earth, Hammond was promoted to the rank of lieutenant general and offered a position as the head of a new department at the Pentagon unofficially entitled Homeworld Security. In his new role, Hammond was entrusted with the oversight of all things related to Earth's defense including the facility in Antarctica, the BC-303 program, and the SGC, where General O'Neill had replaced him. When Hammond accepted command of the *Prometheus* mission to Atlantis, he chose to lead the mission himself, and although the ship was hijacked and diverted by Vala without reaching its destination, *Prometheus* was recovered and safely returned, and a second mission was planned.

Prometheus

MILITARY DECORATIONS

General Hammond is a highly decorated officer whose meritorious service in Vietnam, Kuwait, and Stargate Command has spanned nearly 40 years. His strength, loyalty, and wisdom have earned him the respect of those with whom he has served.

Master Space/Missile Badge, command level

Command Pilot Badge, command level

Legion of Merit, 2nd Award

Meritorious Service Medal, 4th Award

Air Force Outstanding Unit Award, 4th Award

Air Force Commendation Medal, 4th Award

Combat Rediness Medal

Vietnam Service Medal, 2nd Award

Southwest Asia Service Medal, 2nd Award

Air Force Longevity Service Award, 6th Award

Air Medal, 9th Award

Distinguished Flying Cross

Defense Meritorious Service Medal

Joint Service Commendation Medal

Air Force Organizational Excellence Award

National Defense Service Medal, 2nd Award

Air Force Overseas Ribbon—Short Tour

Air Force Training Ribbon

Air Force Overseas Ribbon—Long Tour

Kuwait Liberation Medal, Kingdom of Saudi Arabia, with Palm

Republic of Vietnam Gallantry Cross

Air Force Small arms Expert Ribbon

Republic of Vietnam Campaign Medal

Dr. Janet Fraiser

AS THE CHIEF MEDICAL OFFICER of the SGC, Dr. Fraiser was responsible for the health and well being of all SGC personnel. An accomplished surgeon and practiced diagnostician, she was also highly respected as a specialist in both exotic diseases and alien physiology. As both a skilled physician and a dedicated military officer, she was guided by her deep compassion, her unyielding principles, and her fierce determination to protect those in her care.

Dr. Fraiser's compassion extended to all patients, both ally and enemy, human and alien.

TRAINING

Dr. Fraiser was hand selected for her expertise in exotic diseases. She was frequently called upon to conduct medical research and analysis of unknown contagions, and to examine, heal, and cure a variety of alien organisms and life-forms. From her experience at SGC, she became arguably the planet's foremost authority on alien species.

FAMILY

Dr. Fraiser had been married to a man who did not understand or approve of her joining the Air Force, and she had remained single since her divorce. Following the mission to Hanka, she adopted Cassandra, the 12 year old refugee who was the only survivor of her planet, and she raised her daughter as a devoted single mother.

Cassandra had become a victim of Nirrti's genetic experiments.

FACT FILE

INJURIES IN THE LINE OF DUTY
Dr. Fraiser's position often put her at risk for injury or infection. She was exposed to the Reol chemical, contracted an Ancient virus, and was infected by Ma'chello's inventions. She was duplicated by the aliens of P3X-118, deflected by Osiris's ribbon device, and suffered a bullet wound during the battle with Hathor. On P3X-666, her courage under fire saved the life of Airman Wells even as she lost her own life to a staff weapon blast. At Dr. Fraiser's memorial service, Carter honored her memory by naming the numerous men and women whose lives she had saved. "We often talk about those that give their lives in the service of their country, and while Janet Fraiser did just that, that's not what her life was about. The following are the names of the men and women who did not die in service, but who are in fact alive today, because of Janet..."

When Hathor seized control of the SGC, Fraiser was injured when she was shot in the arm.

When on a mission to Egypt, Fraiser was deflected by Osiris's ribbon device.

Carter remembered those whose lives were touched by Janet Fraiser.

OFF-WORLD MISSIONS
Dr. Fraiser's role as a physician occasionally took her through the stargate to off-world planets and cultures. Following the contagion that had wiped out the population of Hanka, she visited the planet to set up quarantine conditions, attend to those who had been exposed, and to assure that the infection did not spread. During the mission to PJ2-445, she investigated the illness being spread among the humanoid aliens and helped to identify and reverse its cause. She also joined the mission to the Alpha Site to assist in the treatment of wounded refugees.

A mysterious ailment on PJ2-445 affected both the native humanoid aliens and the members of SG-1.

P3X-666
When SG-13 was ambushed on P3X-666, Dr. Fraiser was sent to the planet as part of the rescue mission. Airman Simon Wells had been critically wounded by a staff weapon, and Dr. Fraiser treated him in the field under heavy weapons fire. Through her heroic efforts she was able to stabilize the young airman, however Dr. Fraiser lost her own life during the battle, the victim of a staff weapon blast to the chest. Simon Wells survived his wound and was able to return home for the birth of his first child, a daughter whom he named Janet, in honor of Dr. Janet Fraiser.

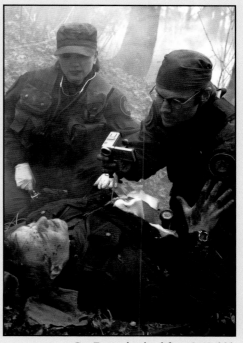

Dr. Fraiser lost her life on P3X-666.

PROMOTIONS
Dr. Fraiser entered the SGC as a captain. Her outstanding dedication earned her a number of commendations, and after three and a half years of exemplary service, she was promoted to the rank of major. As Chief Medical Officer, however, Dr. Fraiser was responsible for all base personnel, and in medical matters she overruled those of any rank.

MILITARY DECORATIONS
In addition to being a skilled physician, Dr. Fraiser was also an outstanding military officer. She was recommended for a commendation following her actions in helping to defeat Hathor on the base, and she was decorated for her courage and heroism.

Medical Corps. Senior Level Badge

Air Force Commendation Medal, 2nd Award
National Defense Service Medal
Air Force Achievement Medal
Air Force Outstanding Unit Award
Air Force Overseas Ribbon —Short Tour
Air Force Longevity Service Award, 3rd Award
Air Force Training Ribbon
Southwest Asia service Medal, 2nd Award
Kuwait Liberation Medal, Kingdom of Saudi Arabia, with Palm

STARGATE COMMAND

Stargate Command

STARGATE COMMAND, or SGC, was established through a presidential directive in 1997 and initially known only to the President and Joint Chiefs of Staff. Teams operate on a covert basis out of sublevel 28 of Cheyenne Mountain, with standing orders to seek new allies and procure technologies. The top secret program, costing $7.4 billion annually, is classified under Section 11-C-9 of the National Security Act, and is routinely described using the cover story of analysis of deep space radar telemetry.

The briefing room at Stargate Command

AREA 52
The Pentagon designated the unofficial line item referring to the Stargate Program as Area 52.

ALPHA SITE
The Alpha Site is the SGC's off-world base. P3X-984 was chosen as the first location for the site because its address was unknown to the Goa'uld, however when Anubis accessed Jonas's knowledge, the location was compromised and the stargate was transported to a new planet. Despite precautions, the new location came under attack and the self-destruct was engaged. Afterwards, the Alpha Site was relocated to P4X-650 where the new base was built inside a mountain, much like the SGC.

SECURITY LOCKDOWN
Various levels of coded emergencies are used in the event of invasion or containment failure. A security breach often requires a Code Foxtrot Alpha Six. A Code 9 lockdown requires that the base be quarantined, and in the event of containment failure, the Wildfire Directive activates automatically.

AUTODESTRUCT SEQUENCE
The autodestruct sequence is used as a failsafe measure to destroy the SGC complex in the event that security lockdown procedures fail.

1:37
AUTODESTRUCT IN PROGRESS

AUTHORIZATION CODES
Security protocols demand that special authorization codes be entered into the computer.

SIGNAL CODE
7 0 6 2 9 5 7
0 2 8 2 0 0 2
SIGNAL ANALYZED

The beta stargate had been stored at Area 51.

AREA 51

The Groom Lake Facility in the Nevada desert at Nellis Air Force Base, known as Area 51, is the top secret base where all technology brought back through the stargate is sent for study and development. Recovered artifacts and technology housed there have included the quantum mirror, symbiote poison, mimic devices, and the Ancient spacecraft and time travel device. Despite strict precautions, the facility has been plagued by security breaches, and some artifacts and research have been stolen by rogue agents of the Committee and the Trust for commercial application and profit. Among the legitimate developments to come out of Area 51 are the X-301, X-302, and X-303 series of human-built spacecraft, upon which most of the current research is focusing.

White Rock Insignia

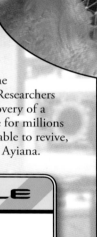

WHITE ROCK RESEARCH STATION

The White Rock Research Station was established in Antarctica immediately after the discovery of the beta stargate. Researchers there made the incredible discovery of a young woman frozen in the ice for millions of years, whom they were able to revive, and whom they named Ayiana.

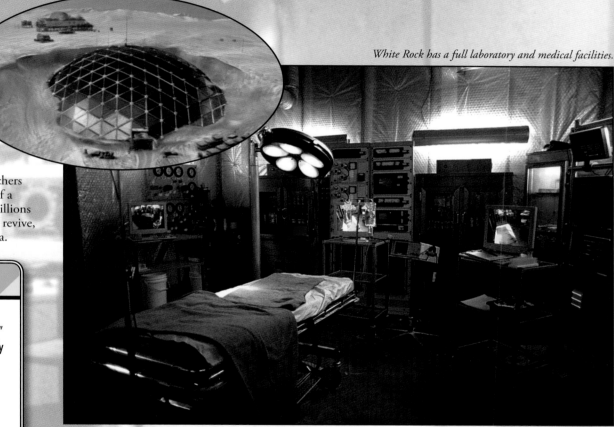

White Rock has a full laboratory and medical facilities.

FACT FILE

DEFCON

DEFCON is short for "DEFense Readiness CONditions," and outlines progressive alert postures used primarily by the Joint Chiefs of Staff. DEFCON 1 was reached during Anubis's attack on Earth.

DEFCON 5: Normal peacetime readiness

DEFCON 4: Normal, increased intelligence and strengthened security measures

DEFCON 3: Increase in force readiness above normal readiness

DEFCON 2: Further increase in force readiness, but less than maximum readiness

DEFCON 1: Maximum force readiness

INTERNATIONAL DISCLOSURE

Through both deliberate disclosure and unintentional security leaks, the stargate program has come to the attention of certain allies as well as enemies. Faced with Anubis's rise to power, the United States sought international cooperation and invited Russia, Britain, China, France, and later Canada to form a coalition to defend Earth.

Cheyenne Mountain

CHEYENNE MOUNTAIN Complex in Colorado Springs, Colorado was formerly a high security missile silo dating back to the 1960s. The facility now houses NORAD on the main levels, and Stargate Command occupies 13 of the 28 sublevels below. The stargate is housed on sublevel 28. The ceiling retracts, and above the gate is a shaft, remaining from the days as a missile silo, which leads to the surface. A crane mechanism within the shaft is able to hoist the gate up or down.

SECURITY CLEARANCE

Within the facility, security clearance increases with successive sublevels, and the doorways and the lighting in the tunnel hallways use a system of color coding that helps to identify various levels.

NORAD

NORAD, the North American Aerospace Defense Command on the main level at Cheyenne Mountain, is a partnership of Canadian and American military who have protected the airspace over North America since 1958.

CHEYENNE MOUNTAIN COMPLEX

	Level	Door Color	Tunnel Lights	
INTERFACE TO THE OUTSIDE WORLD General Security Military and Civilian Personnel	1	Red	White	Shipping/Receiving
	2		Red	Transport/Vehicle Maintenance
	3		Red	Commissary, Mess Hall
	4		Red	Supplies/Storage
	5		Red	Storage/Loading Dock
	6		White	Security Clearance
FACILITY SUPPORT Medium Security Military Personnel Only	7	Yellow	Yellow	Offices
	8		Yellow	Offices
	9		Yellow	Facility Maintenance/Mechanical
	10		Amber	Earth Based Communications
	11		Amber	Personnel/Records
	12		Amber	
	13		Pale Green	
	14		Pale Green	
	15		Pale Green	
STARGATE PROJECT SUPPORT High Security SGC Personnel	16	White	White	SGC Security/Holding Rooms; Video Surveillance/Isolation Rooms
	17		Pale Blue	Negotiating room
	18		Pale Blue	Daniel's and Jonas's Lab
	19	Turquoise	Pale Blue	Carter's Lab
	20	Dark Blue	Blue	MRI Room; Surveillance; Observation Lab
	21	Medium Blue	Blue	Infirmary/Medical Lab/Operating Theater; Observation Room; Supply Room
	22	Light Blue	Blue	Dr. Fraiser's Office; Isolation Wing; Quarters; General Purpose
	23		Green	Storage Room
	24		Green	
	25	Green	Green	Teal'c's Quarters; Crew and Guest Quarters; Locker Room/Gym
STARGATE PROJECT SUPPORT High Level Security SGC Personnel Only	26		White	Off-world Communications
	27		White	Briefing room; General's office; SGC offices
	28		White	Gateroom; Control Room; Gear Room; Short Term Brig; Armory

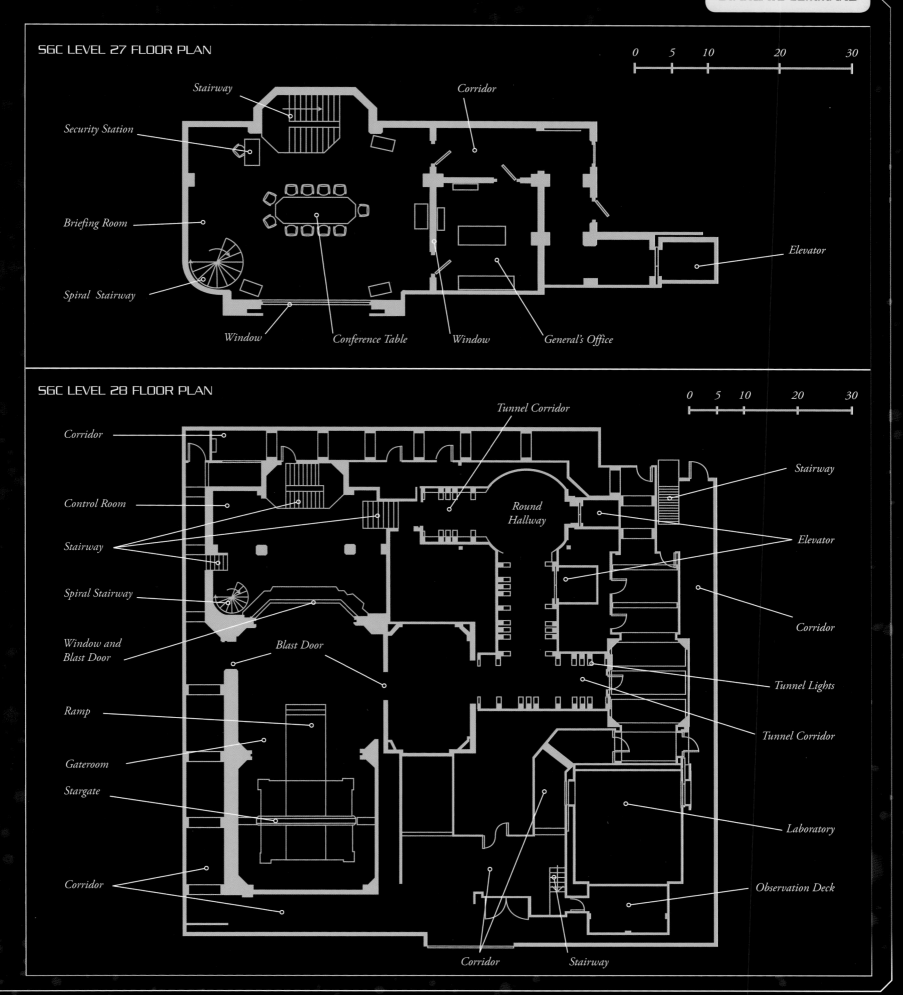

SGC LEVEL 27 FLOOR PLAN

0   5   10   20   30

Stairway

Corridor

Security Station

Briefing Room

Spiral Stairway

Elevator

Window

Conference Table

Window

General's Office

SGC LEVEL 28 FLOOR PLAN

0   5   10   20   30

Corridor

Tunnel Corridor

Control Room

Stairway

Round Hallway

Elevator

Stairway

Spiral Stairway

Corridor

Window and Blast Door

Blast Door

Tunnel Lights

Ramp

Tunnel Corridor

Gateroom

Stargate

Laboratory

Corridor

Observation Deck

Corridor

Stairway

SGC Base Personnel

STARGATE COMMAND serves both as a military base for the defense of the planet and as a research facility for the advancement of discoveries brought back through the stargate. The personnel stationed on the base fulfill vital administrative and scientific roles in support of the teams in the field, including the maintenance and operation of the stargate systems, negotiations with alien cultures, the study of recovered artifacts, and research and development of new technologies.

Dr. Bill Lee

ELIZABETH WEIR

Dr. Elizabeth Weir is a civilian expert on international politics and a skilled negotiator. Due to political pressure, President Hayes asked Dr. Weir to take temporary command of the SGC, and her judgment and shrewd diplomatic skills earned her the respect of SG-1. When General O'Neill took command of the base, Dr. Weir was asked to supervise the Ancient outpost in Antarctica where research would eventually lead to the discovery of the Lost City of Atlantis.

BILL LEE

Dr. Bill Lee, a scientist based at the SGC, has also conducted research off-world on the missions to M4C-862 and P5X-777. He accompanied Daniel to Honduras in search of Telchak's reanimation device and was called to Los Angeles to disarm the naquadah bomb in Sekhmet's ark. His work has led to a number of discoveries including a new ceramic polymer SG vest, the adaptation of the virtual reality chair from P7J-989 as a viable training tool, and research into the potential of a particularly prolific plant from P6J-908.

JAY FELGER

Dr. Jay Felger holds four post-graduate degrees, yet despite his brilliant scientific mind, he is impulsive, clumsy, and socially inept. He idolizes the members of SG-1, and when on a joint mission he witnessed SG-1's capture, he attempted an unauthorized two-man rescue mission. With Carter, he developed Avenger, a computer virus designed to target a specific stargate, however Ba'al's modification of his virus instead caused the entire stargate network to shut down.

Felger on an undercover rescue mission.

WALTER HARRIMAN

Master Sergeant Norman Walter Davis Harriman is one of several specially trained technicians responsible for controlling the stargate computers. His responsibilities usually involve managing communications, iris control, and gate dialing sequences from the control room, as well as serving as an administrative assistant to the general. However, he has also proven himself to be skilled at manning the communications, navigation, sensors, shields, and weapons systems onboard the *Prometheus*, and he has demonstrated an impressive ability to fly an alkesh.

SLY SILER

Sergeant Sly Siler is a technician known for his expertise in the mechanical and electrical operation of the stargate. He frequently cooperates with other base technicians, notably Major Wood, and he is regularly called upon to make corrections and repairs to the stargate systems and equipment, a job which often requires the use of a very big wrench. He has had his share of injuries in the performance of his duties, including severe electrical burns, a broken arm, concussion, broken nose, eye injury, neck injury, and staff weapon burns, but his vital contributions have included repairing the stargate, preparing the MALP and UAV, testing new technology, defending the base, and helping Carter to restore her motorcycle.

RODNEY MCKAY

Dr. Rodney McKay, a brilliant but arrogant physicist, had studied the stargate for over a year from Area 51, and he was called to the SGC when Teal'c was trapped within the stargate matrix. He consistently challenged Carter's theories concerning wormhole physics, but he later assisted Carter in finding a way to counteract Anubis's Ancient weapon which threatened to destroy Earth. His plan to use an electromagnetic pulse generator ultimately failed, but he cooperated with Carter's plan to use the X-302 to launch the stargate away from Earth to be detonated harmlessly in space.

SGC Teams

FOLLOWING THE SECOND ABYDOS mission, the President ordered the formation of nine SG teams whose duties would be to perform reconnaissance, determine threats, and if possible, to make peaceful contact with the peoples of other worlds. A presidential directive later expanded the orders to evaluate the scientific and cultural value of each mission. The overall mandate of stargate missions is to seek new allies and procure technologies to aid in the defense against the Goa'uld or other alien aggressors, and the teams operate on a covert top secret basis from Cheyenne Mountain.

*SG-1,
O'Neill, Teal'c,
Daniel, and Carter*

SG-1, the flagship team of the SGC

As the Stargate Program grew, additional teams were added. By the seventh year, more than 20 SG teams had been established. The flagship team, designated SG-1, under the command of Colonel Jack O'Neill, included Captain Samantha Carter and Dr. Daniel Jackson, with the later additions of Teal'c, and Jonas Quinn.

SG-2

SG-1 has encountered Kawalsky in alternate realities.

SG-2 CHARLES KAWALSKY

Charles Kawalsky was a longtime comrade of O'Neill, and he served under Colonel O'Neill during both missions to Abydos. As a major, he was given command of the newly formed SG-2 unit for the mission to Chulak, but during the battle on the planet he was taken as a host by a larval Goa'uld. By the time his condition was realized, the Goa'uld had already become one with the host, and surgery to remove the symbiote failed. Kawalsky died when the Goa'uld tried to escape through the stargate and he was caught in an event horizon as it disengaged.

*Kawalsky served with
O'Neill in Operation
East Fly, 198.*

*Major Ferretti took command
of SG-2 following the death
of Major Kawalsky.*

SG-2 LOUIS FERRETTI

Major Ferretti participated in both missions to Abydos. He was badly injured in a firefight with Apophis's Jaffa, but was able to identify the dialing symbols which led SG-1 to the first mission to Chulak.

SG-2 COLONEL PIERCE

As a member of SG-2, Pierce had joined the mission to P3X-888. At the rank of major, he took command of SG-15, and following a promotion to colonel, Pierce was placed in command of the Alpha Site on P4X-650.

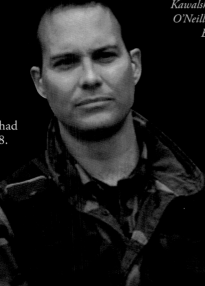

SG-2 MAJOR COBURN

Major Coburn has served as the commanding officer of SG-2, offering backup to SG-1 on the mission to seek the Harsesis child on Kheb, and the mission to rescue Daniel on P3X-888.

SG-2 MAJOR GRIFF

Captain Griff served under Major Coburn during the mission to P3X-888. He was later promoted to major and given command of SG-2 where his team often provided backup and support for SG-1.

Both Griff and Pierce have served under Major Coburn.

Griff and SG-2 provided support on P3R-118 and M4C-862.

SG-3

SG-3 COLONEL REYNOLDS

Major Reynolds of the NID had served under Colonel Maybourne at Area 51 before his promotion to colonel and transfer to the SGC. He commanded SG-16 during the mission to Velona, and later became the commanding officer of SG-3. His team supported SG-1 on missions to Vis Uban, Ramius's planet, the Alpha Site, P3X-439, and P2X-887, and they were selected by Hammond for the Prometheus expedition to Atlantis. He also helped to defend the SGC against the incursion of the Replicators. Colonel Reynolds is intensely loyal to O'Neill, even to the point of assembling the men and women of the base in a show of support and a willingness to go to war on O'Neill's order.

Colonel Reynolds has commanded SG-16 and SG-3.

Makepeace commanded the mission to rescue SG-1 from Hathor.

SG-3 MAJOR WARREN

Major Warren has been a member of the SGC since its inception. He served under Kawalsky during the first mission to Chulak. At the rank of major, he has served as the commanding officer of SG-3 during the missions to P3X-775 and Reese's homeworld, and during the foothold incident on the base.

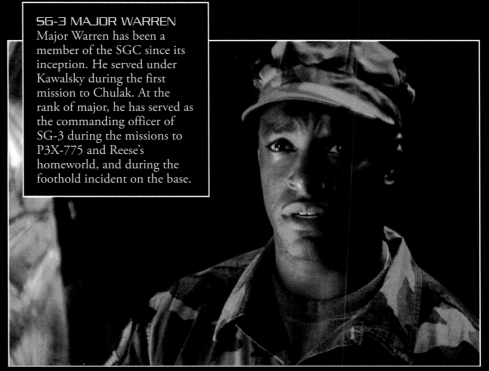

SG-3 COLONEL MAKEPEACE

Colonel Makepeace commanded the SG-3 Marines on P34-353J, the Land of Light, and Hathor's world. When O'Neill's undercover mission to shut down the NID off-world operation exposed Makepeace as a mole, he was arrested for high crimes against the United States.

Warren served on SG-2 under Major Kawalsky during the first mission to Chulak.

SGC Teams

MOST SG TEAMS PERFORM standard recon, but a few also function in specialized capacities. SG-2 and SG-3 perform search and rescue. SG-3 was established as a Marine unit, and SG-4 became Russian. SG-7 is designated scientific and medical, SG-9 diplomatic, and SG-11 deals with science, engineering, and archaeology. A special training program in conjunction with the Air Force Academy prepares qualified graduates as new recruits into the Stargate Program.

SG-11

SG-11 COLONEL EDWARDS
Colonel Edwards, commander of SG-11, headed the naquadah mining survey on P3X-403. When his team came under attack by the native Unas, Edwards prepared to use force in retaliation.

SG-11 CAPTAIN CONNER
The only surviving member of SG-9 under Jonas Hanson, Lieutenant Conner was promoted to captain and commanded SG-11 during the mission to the Salish world of PXY-887.

SG-11 MAJOR LORNE
Major Lorne served under Colonel Edwards on P3X-403 and headed one of the search parties that located Lieutenant Ritter after he had been killed by the Unas.

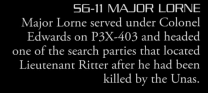

SG-11 LIEUTENANT RITTER
While recording map elevations on P3X-403, Lieutenant Ritter was captured by the Unas and brutally killed.

Lorne coordinated mining surveys for SG-11.

SG-13

SG-13 COLONEL DIXON
Colonel David Dixon commanded SG-13 during the mission to P3X-666 where his team survived an ambush by the Jaffa.

SG-13 DR. BALINSKY
On a mission to P3X-666, SG-13 found the ruins of an Ancient city, a discovery that archaeologist Dr. Balinsky greeted with an enthusiasm reminiscent of Daniel Jackson.

SG-13 BOSWORTH

Bosworth served under Colonel Dixon during the mission to P3X-666. When the team was ambushed and Simon Wells was wounded, Bosworth stayed with his teammate until medical assistance arrived. Bosworth later served under Colonel Reynolds as a member of SG-3 during the Prometheus expedition to Atlantis.

Senior Airman Simon Wells

In an alternate timeline created when history changed, Bosworth joined the first mission to Chulak.

SG-13 SIMON WELLS

Senior Airman Simon Wells and his wife Marci were expecting their first child. During SG-13's mission to P3X-666, the team was ambushed by Jaffa, and Wells was critically wounded in the back by a staff weapon. As he was treated in the field by Dr. Fraiser, he begged Daniel to record his final message to his wife, and Daniel's camera captured the death of Janet Fraiser. Wells survived his wound and returned home in time for the birth of his daughter, whom he named Janet.

Marci Wells and Janet Wells

SG-TRAINEES

Air Force Academy graduates complete special training scenarios before joining the SGC.

LIEUTENANT ELLIOT

Lieutenant Elliot graduated from the SGC's special training program and was assigned to SG-17. On his first mission he was critically wounded on Revanna and taken as a host by Lantash. He volunteered to sacrifice himself to allow SG-1 to escape.

LIEUTENANT HAILEY

Jennifer Hailey was a brilliant but rebellious cadet at the Air Force Academy when Carter allowed her to participate in SG-1's mission to M4C-862. She graduated with areas of expertise in physics and computers and later completed the SGC training scenarios under O'Neill.

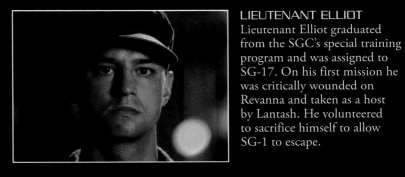

LIEUTENANT GROGAN

Lieutenant Grogan graduated from the Air Force Academy's training program and was assigned to SG-9 under Major Benton. He participated in the diplomatic mission to Latona but was the only member of his team to survive Svarog's attack.

LIEUTENANT SATTERFIELD

Lieutenant Satterfield, an Air Force Academy graduate, completed the special training scenarios under O'Neill to be accepted as a member of the SGC. Her areas of expertise include archaeology and languages, including the ability to read Goa'uld.

Uniforms and Insignia

UNIFORMS WORN BY SG TEAMS are based on regulation Air Force dress. Battle dress uniforms, or "BDUs," are the most common mode of dress both on the base and off-world and are available in several colors including green, blue, forest camouflage, and desert camouflage. The Command usually dictates the prescribed or alternate dress choices, despite Carter's remark that "We call each other every morning."

GREEN BDUs
Green is the most commonly worn color for BDUs, both for the over-shirt, typically used on base, and the heavier jacket, often worn off-world. Forest camouflage is frequently worn off-world by the SG-3 Marines.

SG-1 Emblem

Cotton Jacket

DESERT CAMOUFLAGE BDUS
BDUs of different styles, colors, and fabrics are available for varying climate zones, depending on the need for camouflage. The lighter weight camouflage BDUs, including the coordinating vest, are usually worn in hot or desert climates.

Desert Camo Cap

Sunglasses

Desert Camo Vest

Radio

SGC Earth Emblem

Water Flask

BLUE BDUs
On base, team members often have a choice of color. Blue BDUs with the black T-shirt may be worn on base but are rarely used during off-world missions.

SGC Earth Emblem

SG-1 Emblem

Cotton Jacket

SG VEST

The vest worn by SG teams on most off-world missions is specially designed to carry necessary gear, including the radio. Attempts to use Kevlar or bulletproof armor in the vest had proved ineffective as protection against the energy plasma from a staff weapon blast, but eventually Dr. Lee developed a new ceramic polymer material that resists heat, stops the blast, and fits into a standard-issue SG vest. The new vest saved O'Neill's life during the battle on P3X-666.

SGC Emblem

SGC Earth Emblem

SG-1 Emblem

SG Vest

Radio

Name Badge

Protective Over-Garment

Removable Hood

HAZMAT

Hazmat, a shortened term for "Hazardous Materials," refers to the policies and procedures put in place to deal with dangerous biological or chemical agents. Mission Oriented Protective Posture (MOPP) outlines five levels of protection from MOPP0 to MOPP4, the highest level requiring that an over-garment, helmet cover, vinyl over-boot, mask, hood, and gloves all be worn. The SGC hazmat gear, often brought on off-world missions, may also include a portable oxygen supply for up to 12 hours of protection.

OFFICER RANK INSIGNIA:

Second Lieutenant Rank O-1

Colonel Rank O-6

First Lieutenant Rank O-2

Brigadier General Rank O-7

Captain Rank O-3

Major General Rank O-8

Major Rank O-4

Lieutenant General Rank O-9

Lieutenant Colonel Rank O-5

General Rank O-10

General of the Air Force
Reserved for wartime only

RADIO

SG teams maintain radio contact with each other while off-world and can remain in contact with the SGC by using the antenna of the MALP or UAV to relay the signal through an open wormhole. The radios are equipped with an RDF (radio direction finding) signal that can determine the location of another radio transmission. The designation "niner," for example "SG-1 niner," refers to the commanding officer of the given SG unit.

Weapons

DURING EARLY OFF-WORLD MISSIONS, O'Neill and Carter carried the MP-5 submachine gun. Since the mission to P3X-888, the P-90 has replaced the MP-5 due to its superior performance against the Unas or Jaffa armor. O'Neill and Daniel also carry the Beretta 92R pistol, and Carter and Teal'c have preferred the zat'nik'tel as a sidearm.

MP-5
SUBMACHINE GUN
Standard issue personal defense weapon used from year 1 to 4

Muzzle

Scope

Handle/Stock

Magazine

HK SL8
SNIPER RIFLE
Has been used by O'Neill for specialized sniper fire

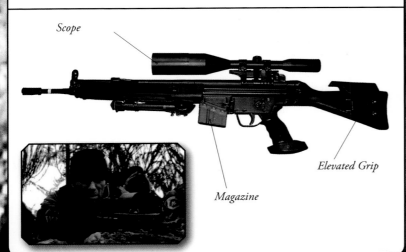

Scope

Elevated Grip

Magazine

P-90
SUBMACHINE GUN
Standard issue personal defense weapon used from year 4 onward

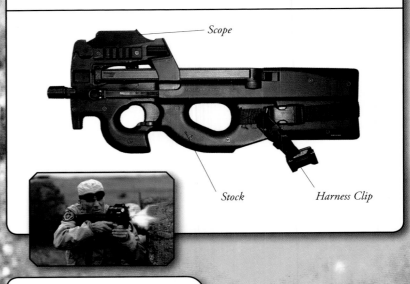

Scope

Stock

Harness Clip

USAS 12
AUTOMATIC SHOTGUN
Especially effective against Replicators

Muzzle

Receiver

Drum Magazine

M60 E3
MEDIUM MACHINEGUN
Belt-fed drum, used during the ambush of a Kull Warrior

Muzzle

Gas Chamber

Handle/Stock

Ammo Belt Bucket

BERETTA 92R
SEMIAUTOMATIC SIDEARM
Standard SGC sidearm carried by O'Neill and Daniel

Slide

SPAS 12
SEMIAUTOMATIC SHOTGUN
Especially effective against Replicators

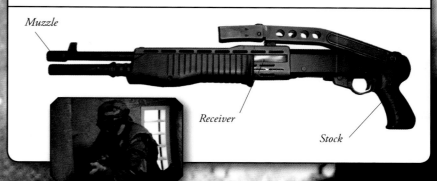

Muzzle

Receiver

Stock

MICRO 16
ASSAULT RIFLE
AKA "Carter Special", customized from M16 and M4 during year 7

Front Stock

Scope

C-Magazine

Alien Weapons

TER
The TER, or Transphase Eradication Rod, is Goa'uld technology created to defeat the Reetou, which are invisible in our phase. The TER compensates for phase-shifting, making the Reetou or cloaked enemies visible in our phase and terminating them. The SGC has acquired the weapons from the Tok'ra.

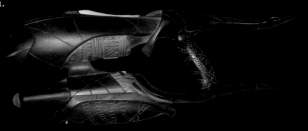

IN'TAR
In'tars are technology acquired from the Goa'uld. They can take the form of common Earth weapons, but are identifiable by the glowing red crystal power source at the base. In'tars are only meant to stun, although they can be adjusted for different intensities, and they have been used in SGC training scenarios.

M249 SAW
LIGHT MACHINEGUN
Squad Automatic Weapon, core combat weapon especially against Jaffa

Handle/Stock

Stock

Belt-fed Magazine

WING CANNON
The wing cannon is the primary weapons system of the death glider. SG-1 created a makeshift weapon by cannibalizing the wing-mounted weapon from a downed death glider, creating a shoulder mounted energy weapon with the power of a death glider and the mobility of a staff weapon.

Earth Technology

W HEN STARGATE teams first
ventured through the gate, they relied
on technology to assess planetary conditions,
determine the viability of the off-world DHD, and
communicate with Stargate Command. The exploration of
other worlds has vastly expanded the technology available to
the SGC, and alien alliances as well as research and development
have led to the advancement of weapons, medicines, and
entire fleets of ships capable of interstellar travel.

Front Claw

Forward Arm

Satellite Dish

Video Camera

Forward Sensor

MALP

The MALP, or Mobile Analytic Laboratory Probe, is an
unmanned, mobile, remote controlled vehicle capable of
assessing off-world environmental conditions and possible
threats before a team is sent through the stargate. The SGC
has many such devices, which are routinely used as
reconnaissance probes and which maintain contact
with the SGC by sending and receiving
audio, video, and radio
transmissions bi-directionally
through the open wormhole.

UTD

The UTD, or Universal
Tricorder Device, is a small,
hand-held device capable of
recognizing a variety of
environmental and
energy signatures.

Light

UTD

Towing Anchor

Armor Plating

All-Terrain Tires

UAV

The UAV, or Unmanned Airborne Vehicle, is a remote controlled
airborne device which can assess planetary conditions when a
manned or MALP mission would be unsuitable. It has a range of
several miles, and can be set to fly an automatic search pattern or
be controlled remotely from the SGC through an open wormhole.
The UAV can function as a means of off-world communication
by relaying bi-directional audio/video transmissions, and it has
been used for aerial reconnaissance, search and rescue, and
weapons guidance. It can also be equipped with missiles
that can be fired by remote control.

FRED
The Field Remote Expeditionary Device transport vehicle was replaced by the more versatile MALP.

Manual Throttle

Safety Railing

Engine Grill

X-301
The X-301 Interceptor was an experimental hybrid craft built by a team of SGC engineers using an American design and two recovered Goa'uld death gliders. Intended as a platform from which to launch an attack against a Goa'uld mothership, the two-man craft was equipped with stealth technology and two AIM-120A air-to-air missiles. However, the death gliders used in its construction had been sabotaged by a hidden recall device which activated during its test flight and sent the X-301 craft hurtling into deep space. It had to be abandoned after the rescue of pilots O'Neill and Teal'c.

X-301

X-302
The X-302 was designed at Area 51 following the failure of the X-301, and was intended to be the first manmade craft capable of both aerial combat and interstellar travel.

F-302
When the experimental X-302 was added to the U.S. Air Force fleet, it became officially known as the fighter craft, F-302. A space-worthy fighter-interceptor aircraft retro-engineered from Goa'uld technology but entirely human-built, the F-302 has four different sets of engines: air-breathing jets, modified aerospikes for high altitudes, a rocket booster, and a naquadria-powered hyperspace window generator, although it has only been able to engage the hyperdrive engines in short controlled bursts due to continuing problems with the instability of naquadria. Earth now commands a fleet of F-302s, and the ships have been used in the defense of the planet including the elimination of the sabotaged beta stargate, the mission to disable Anubis's superweapon, and the battle over Antarctica. Specially trained F-302 pilots have adopted the nickname "Snakeskinners," and while both Teal'c and Carter are experienced F-302 pilots, O'Neill is considered to be the foremost F-302 pilot on the planet.

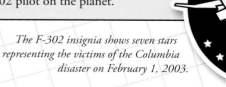

The F-302 insignia shows seven stars representing the victims of the Columbia disaster on February 1, 2003.

X-303
The X-303 prototype, codenamed *Prometheus*, was the third in a series of human designs incorporating key alien systems and technology, and was built as a countermeasure to the Goa'uld mothership.

Prometheus

THE PROMETHEUS, the prototype of the X-303 class of Earth-built vessels, was constructed at Area 51 over a period of approximately two years in a project that was so secret the government appropriated the budget of several billion dollars without the usual congressional oversight. When the experimental craft became a part of Earth's fleet, it became officially known as the battle cruiser BC-303, the United States Air Force Vessel *Prometheus*. The *Prometheus* was succeeded by the next generation of interstellar ships including the *Daedalus*.

O'Neill wanted to name the X-303 "Enterprise."

DESIGN

The *Prometheus* is constructed of naquadah and a trinium alloy. Many of its key systems use crystal technology rather than wires and chips, and its design includes the most advanced scanning and weapons technology available. The ship is equipped with a ring transporter which can be used to enter and exit the vessel as it hovers above a planet, and it is also able to land on a planet's surface. Inertial dampeners and artificial gravity limit the effect of G-forces and zero gravity.

The bridge of the Prometheus.

Naquadah and trinium alloy construction.

NID HIJACKING

Before the *Prometheus* was completed, it became the target of a hijacking plot by rogue NID agents who planned to use the ship to reach a cache of weapons and technology described in an Ancient text. Using the cover story of a media leak, four rogue NID operatives commandeered the ship and obtained the release of Colonel Simmons and Adrian Conrad. Both Simmons and Conrad were killed during the failed hijacking attempt, and SG-1 reclaimed the ship 1200 light years from Earth.

Adrian Conrad was killed during the hijacking attempt.

HALA

Because *Prometheus* is vastly inferior to Asgard technology, it was ideally suited to enter Replicator-dominated space, and at Thor's request, SG-1 flew the *Prometheus* to Hala to repair a time-dilation device that would contain the Replicators. In appreciation, Thor added Asgard shields and weapons to the ship's design.

Thor sought SG-1's assistance at Hala.

Prometheus landed on Tagrea for

TAGREA

During *Prometheus*'s shakedown cruise under Colonel Ronson's command, an intense gravity wave shut down the hyperdrive engines. The ship was forced to divert to Tagrea, where the naquadria reactor went critical and was jettisoned, and the crew relied on the Tagrean stargate to return home.

NEBULA

As *Prometheus* returned from Tagrea, it came under attack from an unknown alien vessel and was forced to take cover in a gaseous nebula-like cloud. However, once inside the cloud, the engines could not be engaged, and *Prometheus* was stranded until Carter was able to create a partial shift into hyperspace to extract the ship.

Vala Mal Doran

ANTARCTICA

Newly fitted with Asgard hyperdrive engines and beam technology, *Prometheus* was called upon to defend Earth from Anubis. Under the command of General Hammond, *Prometheus* and its fleet of F-302s engaged Anubis's motherships in battle above Antarctica, allowing SG-1 to launch the Ancient defense weapon.

ATLANTIS

Prometheus's first intergalactic journey was a mission under the command of General Hammond to rendezvous with the Atlantis expedition in the Pegasus galaxy. However, before leaving the galaxy, the ship responded to an apparent distress signal and diverted off course where it was boarded and hijacked by Vala Mal Doran. The ship was recovered, but it had sustained hull damage and returned to Earth for repairs before making another hyperspace journey.

Vala hijacked the ship with Daniel aboard.

Prometheus

USING SUB-LIGHT engines, *Prometheus* can accelerate to more than half the speed of light at 110,000 miles per second, and it is capable of reaching orbit in less than 30 seconds. Equipped with both laser and missile weapons systems, it was also designed to carry a complement of eight F-302 fighters. Asgard modifications, including shields, weapons, and beam technology, have significantly improved the ship's original design, and the unstable naquadria hyperdrive has been replaced by Asgard hyperdrive engines, making *Prometheus* capable of intergalactic travel.

Prometheus *uses laser and missile weapons systems.*

Standard & Deep Space Radar Arrays

Science & Medical Labs (Horseshoe Decks 1 thru 4)

Forward Cargo Hangar

Forward Missile Battery

Bow Sensor

Cargo Storage

Bow Laser Battery

Fuel Storage

Airlock

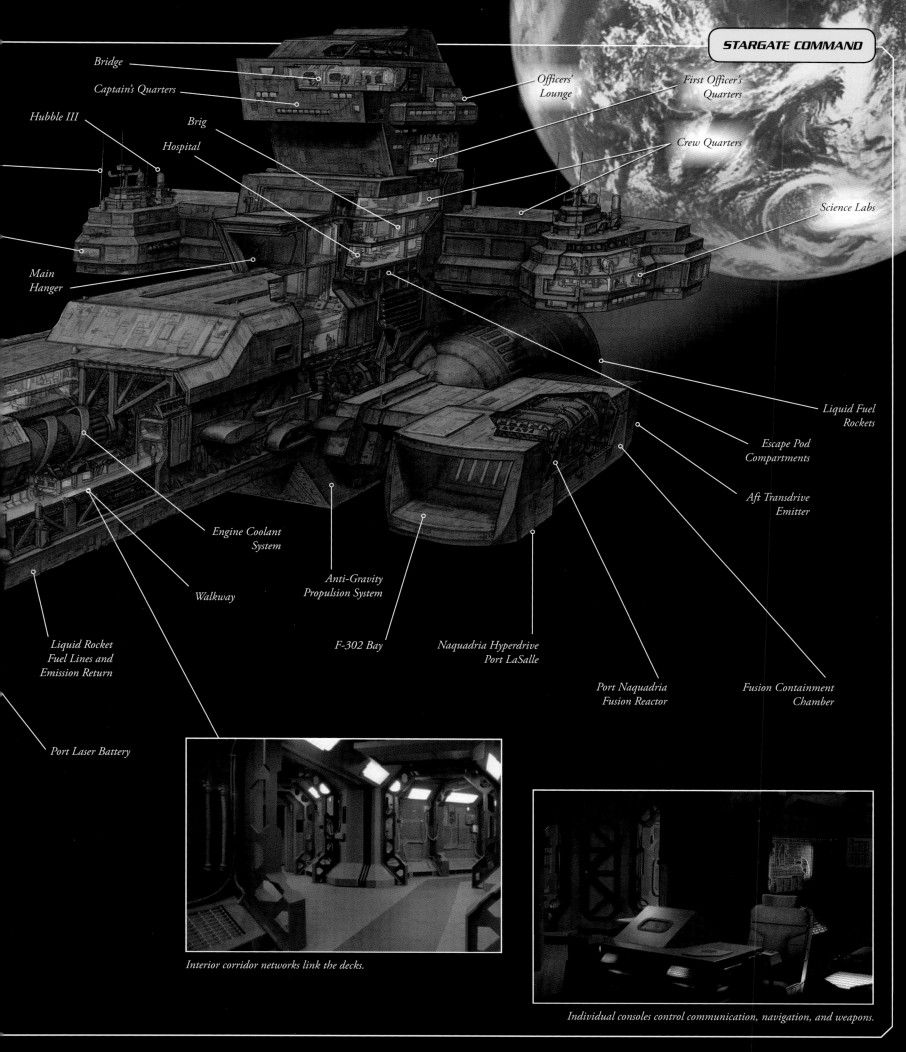

Bridge

Captain's Quarters

Officers' Lounge

First Officer's Quarters

Hubble III

Brig

Hospital

Crew Quarters

Science Labs

Main Hanger

Liquid Fuel Rockets

Escape Pod Compartments

Engine Coolant System

Aft Transdrive Emitter

Walkway

Anti-Gravity Propulsion System

Liquid Rocket Fuel Lines and Emission Return

F-302 Bay

Naquadria Hyperdrive Port LaSalle

Port Naquadria Fusion Reactor

Fusion Containment Chamber

Port Laser Battery

Interior corridor networks link the decks.

Individual consoles control communication, navigation, and weapons.

Alien Technology

EXPLORATION OF THE GALAXY has opened doors to incredible new technologies. Although Earth is still very young by the standards of many advanced races such as the Ancients, the Asgard, and the Goa'uld, encounters with these and other alien races have enabled the SGC to gain new insights and to acquire, modify, and adapt many alien technologies for use on Earth.

Most Goa'uld worlds have a high incidence of naquadah, a substance unknown in our solar system.

NAQUADAH

Naquadah is the element from which the stargate is made. Unknown on Earth, it is an extremely dense, dark gray, quartz-like metal, and the basis of Goa'uld technology and physiology. Naquadah will greatly magnify the explosive energy of nuclear ordinance and is required in the construction of F-302 and BC-303 spacecraft. The SGC seeks off-world naquadah resources for its countless potential military and scientific applications. Certain Goa'uld technologies, such as the ribbon device, require the presence of naquadah in the blood for activation.

NAQUADAH REACTOR

The naquadah reactor is a small but powerful energy source, the technology and plans for which were acquired through a cultural exchange with the planet Orban. Through Carter's modifications, the naquadah reactor, or naquadah generator, has become an efficient and portable energy source which is routinely used by the SGC to interface with alien technology or to power anything from an alien ship to the Alpha Site. Naquadah generator technology was traded to Russia in exchange for borrowing the Russian DHD.

Carter used a naquadah reactor to counteract the cloaking technology of the Ashrak.

STASIS

Stasis chambers, which dramatically slow autonomic functions, have been used by a number of races as a means of prolonging or preserving life. Among the Goa'uld, Osiris, Isis, and Egeria were placed in stasis in canopic jars which could keep a symbiote alive indefinitely. The Eurondans, Hebridans, and people of Talthus have used stasis chambers to allow their populations to survive prolonged journeys or wars. The Tok'ra, Asgard, and Ancients have also used stasis technology for medical and research purposes.

SG-1 was cryogenically frozen with no memory of its capture.

CRYOGENICS

Hathor captured SG-1 and used a system of cryogenic suspension that relied on lowering body temperature to slow autonomic functions and maintain stasis.

The Stromos used stasis chambers for long voyages.

CRYSTALS

Much of alien technology is based on the use of crystals which can function as a power source as well as a means of storing and transmitting information. The Ancients used crystal technology for powering the stargate network and for their most significant power source, the zero point module. The Goa'uld, as scavengers, have also relied on crystal power sources for technology such as the ring transporter, staff weapon, control and hyperdrive systems for their ships, and data storage and retrieval.

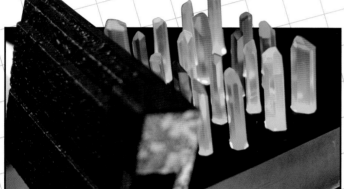

Goa'uld ships use crystal technology.

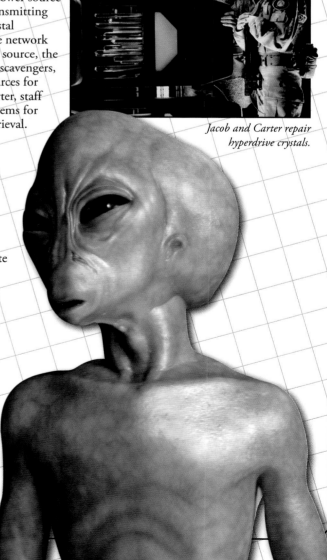

Jacob and Carter repair hyperdrive crystals.

NANO-TECHNOLOGY

Nano-technology is based on microscopic mechanical cell-like units which replicate rather than multiply. SG-1 has encountered many examples of nano-technology in use on other worlds. The Orbanians use nanites as an artificial means of acquiring knowledge, and nano-technology can be used to artificially accelerate ageing as in the case of Shifu or Anna or the nano-virus of Argos. Reese's creator used nano-technology to create an incredibly sophisticated artificial life-form, and Reese used the same technology to create the Replicators.

CLONES

Cloning technology uses genetic material to create an exact duplicate of a living organism. The Asgard reproduce exclusively through enhanced cellular mitosis, and through cloning have achieved a measure of immortality. However, Loki's unsanctioned experiments produced a young clone of Jack O'Neill which failed to age properly. Scientists on Earth have also attempted cloning technology. Colson Industries grew an Asgard clone from a DNA sample, and scientists at Immunitech successfully cloned a Goa'uld symbiote.

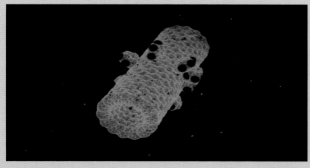

Microscopic nanite

Asgard DNA can grow a clone to maturity in three months.

Alien Technology

REANIMATION DEVICE

The reanimation device was designed as a healing device by the Ancients and later claimed by the Goa'uld Telchak. Capable of reanimating dead tissue, it proved far too powerful for human hosts, and although Telchak modified the technology to create the first sarcophagus, he could not eliminate its negative side effects. The device was hidden in Telchak's temple on Earth, part of the Mayan Fountain of Youth mythology, and Nicholas Ballard's notes later led Daniel to discover the device in the jungles of Honduras.

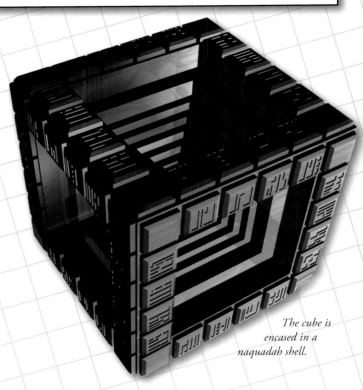

The cube is encased in a naquadah shell.

Anubis used similar reanimation technology to give life to the synthetically created hosts of his Kull Warrior army, and Carter and Jacob were able to analyze the device and engineer a prototype energy weapon, a small power unit, that would counteract its life-giving energy and defeat the Kull Warriors.

ENERGY WEAPON

The energy weapon, or drone weapon, counteracts reanimation technology. It is a small power chip that displays a blue flashing light when activated and clips onto standard firearms such as a P-90 or TER, enabling them to fire a bluish energy beam. The energy weapon is effective against Kull Warriors.

VITUAL REALITY CHAIR

The virtual reality chairs of P7J-989 served to maintain the lives of the planet's surviving residents in suspended animation. Through small puncture wounds in the body, the chairs provide nourishment and channel experience and imagination into and out of the mind. At least two of the chair devices were brought back to the SGC for study, and Dr. Lee worked to modify the technology to be used as a viable training tool for SGC personnel.

TRETONIN

Tretonin is the greatest scientific discovery of the Pangarans, a drug that makes the immune system impervious to any ailment. Pangaran medical experiments had bred symbiotes in captivity in order to synthesize the healing properties of the Goa'uld, however tretonin completely suppressed the normal human immune system, causing a dependence on the drug. The Tok'ra have since refined tretonin specifically for Jaffa physiology, and many Jaffa, including Teal'c and Bra'tac, now live without symbiotes but rely instead on regular doses of tretonin.

Residents remained in suspended animation as their world regenerated itself.

Teal'c volunteered to test the SGC's virtual reality training scenario.

Tretonin was derived from the Goa'uld offspring of a symbiote queen.

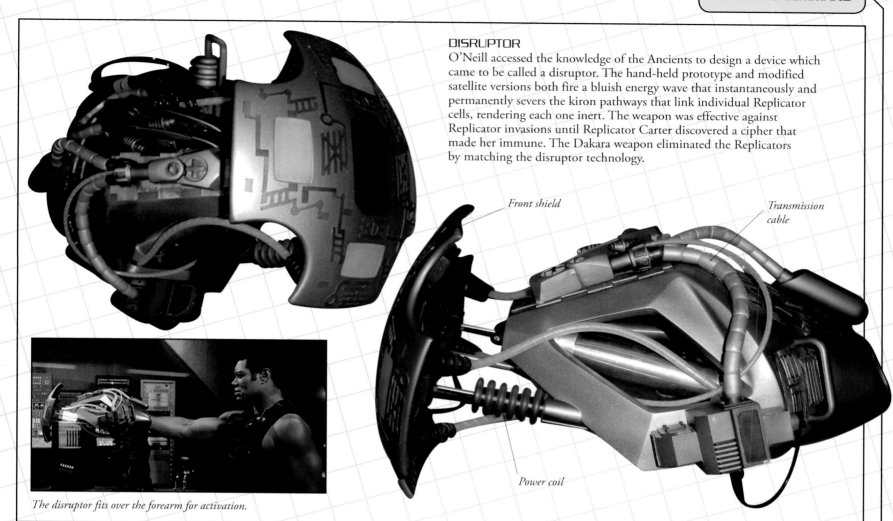

DISRUPTOR

O'Neill accessed the knowledge of the Ancients to design a device which came to be called a disruptor. The hand-held prototype and modified satellite versions both fire a bluish energy wave that instantaneously and permanently severs the kiron pathways that link individual Replicator cells, rendering each one inert. The weapon was effective against Replicator invasions until Replicator Carter discovered a cipher that made her immune. The Dakara weapon eliminated the Replicators by matching the disruptor technology.

Front shield

Transmission cable

Power coil

The disruptor fits over the forearm for activation.

SYMBIOTE POISON

Ren'al, of the Tok'ra, designed a synthetically created toxin that targets symbiotes, a poison that is equally deadly to Goa'uld, Tok'ra, and Jaffa. It was first used on Revanna to eliminate Zipacna's forces, and scientists at Area 51 continued to modify the poison, creating a more stable version that causes instantaneous death but is non-persistent. Although intended as a defensive option, the Trust has used the poison to launch a full-scale chemical attack against Goa'uld-occupied worlds.

The blue liquid dissipates as an invisible gas.

The device is attached near the temple.

A flickering blue light indicates the device is active.

MEMORY RECALL DEVICE

The memory recall device, an example of Tok'ra technology, uses a small round implant near the temple to stimulate and amplify the memory centers of the brain. Although there are no specific ways of exactly targeting certain memories, the device can be adjusted to different levels, from brief flashes to hypnotic recall. When connected to an external device, it can project what the mind's eye is seeing holographically or be used in conjunction with a zatarc detector.

AS A MILITARY OPERATION under the direct command of the President of the United States and the Joint Chiefs of Staff, the SGC was established under the jurisdiction of the Pentagon. The commander of the SGC closely coordinates with the government and the military both for routine missions and for extraordinary situations, and representatives from the Pentagon frequently visit the facility in the role of liaison.

President Hayes remains a strong supporter of the Stargate Program.

PRESIDENT HENRY HAYES

President Hayes was elected to the White House during the seventh year of the Stargate Program, and he has proven himself to be a shrewd strategist. He stood up to Anubis with grit and sarcasm, put his faith in Weir, O'Neill, and SG-1, and launched the *Prometheus* into battle against Anubis under the command of General Hammond. When he learned the truth about the illicit connections of his vice president, Robert Kinsey, he demanded Kinsey's resignation.

RICHARD WOOLSEY

Richard Woolsey of the NID is a brilliant legal mind who was tapped by Senator Kinsey to conduct a full investigation into strategic policy at the SGC. A firm believer in civilian oversight, Woolsey also considers himself to be a man of integrity, and as his suspicions about Kinsey's motivations grew, he turned to General Hammond. He acquired incriminating evidence against Kinsey which he turned over to President Hayes.

AGENT MALCOLM BARRETT

NID Agent Barrett first encountered SG-1 during his mission to detain Martin Lloyd. He remained loyal to the mandates of the NID, even as rogue agents working from within began to support a shadow organization. While under special assignment from the President to expose the cancer in the NID, Barrett worked with Carter and brought about the arrest of members of the Committee. Agent Barrett has collaborated with the SGC on a number of operations including the investigation of Dr. Keffler.

Barrett and SG-1 investigated an NID sleeper cell.

MAJOR PAUL DAVIS

Major Paul Davis, an Air Force officer assigned to the Pentagon, acts as the liaison between the SGC and the Office of the Joint Chiefs of Staff. He has coordinated with the SGC during situations requiring direct contact with the Pentagon, including the black hole incident, the foothold situation, the invasion by Replicators, the recovery of O'Neill and Teal'c from deep space, the asteroid threat, and negotiations with the Russians and foreign dignitaries.

Major Davis acts as a military and diplomatic liaison.

GENERAL VIDRINE

Lieutenant General Vidrine, from the Pentagon, observed the first test flights of the X-301. Impressed by the technology, and supportive of the program, he was later promoted to four stars and placed in charge of the BC-303 program. When naquadah was found on P3X-403, he authorized the use of deadly force, if necessary, to acquire the mineral for BC-303 production.

GENERAL FRANCIS MAYNARD

General Maynard is the Chairman of the Joint Chiefs during the Hayes administration. He briefed the President on his first day in office regarding the existence of the Stargate Program, and he has remained staunchly supportive of the SGC, commending the people there for the number of times they have saved this world.

GENERAL MICHAEL E. RYAN

General Ryan, the Chief of Staff of the U.S. Air Force, visited the SGC to discuss the establishment of a research station on M4C-862.

General Michael E. Ryan

General John P. Jumper

GENERAL JOHN P. JUMPER

General Jumper succeeded General Ryan as the Chief of Staff of the U.S. Air Force, and he counseled President Hayes during Anubis's attack on Earth.

NID and The Trust

The NID, an intelligence organization financed by the government to provide oversight of top secret military operations, is so clandestine that even its full name is unknown. However, philosophical skirmishes concerning the SGC mandate led to the emergence of a shadow organization within the NID. Rogue agents began operating outside the law in cooperation with a covert group of businessmen and political leaders, their goal being the acquisition of alien technology by any means necessary.

Headquartered in Washington, the NID has close ties to the Pentagon and Area 51.

Rogue elements within the NID began covert operations with a unique agenda.

OFF-WORLD OPERATION

Under Colonel Maybourne, several rogue NID teams used the beta stargate on Earth to operate from an off-world base with the express purpose of acquiring alien technology to be stolen or reverse engineered. In a top-secret undercover mission, O'Neill exposed the illegal operation, and rogue operatives were convicted of high treason and sentenced to death row. However, the cancer within the NID had not been eliminated.

Rogue elements established an off-world base of operations.

Coordinates: 38-28-15-35-3-19

ANNA

In an attempt to create a human-Goa'uld hybrid with access to the Goa'uld genetic memory, Dr. Keffler had spliced a human ovum with DNA from the preserved symbiote of the Goa'uld Sekhmet. He named his creation Anna, but as Anna accessed dark memories, Sekhmet unexpectedly began to emerge as a distinct personality. Tortured by a life that held no hope, Anna confronted Keffler, and for the evil he had created in her, she took his life and then her own.

Nano-technology had artificially aged Anna in only three years.

O'Neill infiltrated and exposed the rogue NID operation.

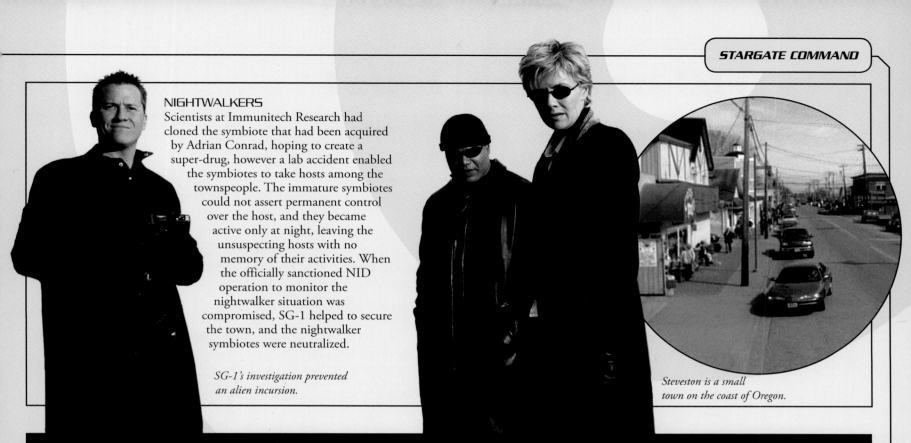

NIGHTWALKERS

Scientists at Immunitech Research had cloned the symbiote that had been acquired by Adrian Conrad, hoping to create a super-drug, however a lab accident enabled the symbiotes to take hosts among the townspeople. The immature symbiotes could not assert permanent control over the host, and they became active only at night, leaving the unsuspecting hosts with no memory of their activities. When the officially sanctioned NID operation to monitor the nightwalker situation was compromised, SG-1 helped to secure the town, and the nightwalker symbiotes were neutralized.

SG-1's investigation prevented an alien incursion.

Steveston is a small town on the coast of Oregon.

THE COMMITTEE

A consortium of private businessmen known as the Committee had invested millions in the acquisition of stolen alien technology for profit. Rogue agents of the NID worked for the Committee, who functioned behind the scenes, and they orchestrated the assassination attempt on Senator Kinsey's life using stolen mimic devices to frame O'Neill for the crime. Agent Barrett and SG-1 exposed and arrested five key members of the Committee, however their covert activities continued.

Brent Langham, Area 51, acquired stolen mimic devices.

Mark Devlin, NID, carried out the assassination attempt.

THE TRUST

Remnants of the Committee and the rogue NID came to be known as the Trust, an enormously powerful and clandestine group with the ability to operate above the law. When fugitive agents were taken as Goa'uld hosts and infiltrated the Russian and American governments, the world was brought to the brink of nuclear annihilation. The Trust continues to be a threat as Goa'uld within the organization remain at large.

Trust operative Jennings

Trust operative Hoskins

The Trust kidnapped Daniel and framed Teal'c in an attempt to acquire Osiris's abandoned alkesh as a base of operations.

65

NID and The Trust

Kinsey's ambitions took him to the White House.

SENATOR ROBERT KINSEY

Since the inception of the SGC, Senator Kinsey has used political posturing and religious rhetoric in an attempt to gain control of the program. When an investigation by O'Neill and Maybourne accumulated evidence of Kinsey's ties to illegal NID activities, he was placed in a vulnerable position. He became a target of the Committee, who orchestrated his assassination, however he survived the attempt and used the incident to his political advantage, acquiring a position on the Intelligence Oversight Committee.

VICE PRESIDENT

Kinsey used his knowledge of the Stargate Program as leverage to propel himself onto the presidential ticket as the running mate of Henry Hayes. Vice President Kinsey renewed his agenda to clean house at the SGC, but, when Richard Woolsey acquired the disk of evidence collected earlier by O'Neill and Maybourne and turned it over to President Hayes, the president demanded Kinsey's resignation.

Kinsey took political advantage of an assassination attempt.

THE TRUST

When Kinsey was abducted by Trust operatives and implanted with a symbiote, he became a pawn in a scheme to ignite a nuclear war. He escaped custody and fled the Trust's alkesh before it was destroyed, and although he is presumed dead, his true fate is unknown.

Simmons investigated Orlin and Lt. Tyler.

COLONEL FRANK SIMMONS

Colonel Simmons, a shadowy figure from the Pentagon, carried out the secret agenda of the NID. He was involved in the oversight of the SGC, and took custody of Adrian Conrad following his implantation as a Goa'uld. Simmons was arrested when O'Neill and Maybourne uncovered incriminating evidence against him, however, when NID operatives hijacked the *Prometheus*, they demanded the release of both Simmons and Conrad. In a struggle on board *Prometheus*, Simmons killed Conrad and was taken as a host by Conrad's symbiote, but was then sucked out of the airlock door and left to die in space.

User 4574

ADRIAN CONRAD

Adrian Conrad, a wealthy industrialist and the head of Zetatron Industries, had been in the late stages of Burchardt's Syndrome, an extremely rare and terminal condition, when he arranged to procure a symbiote as a means to a cure. The implantation procedure was successful, however Conrad, now a Goa'uld, was taken into custody by Colonel Simmons. During the hijacking incident aboard Prometheus, a struggle between Conrad and Simmons left Conrad dead.

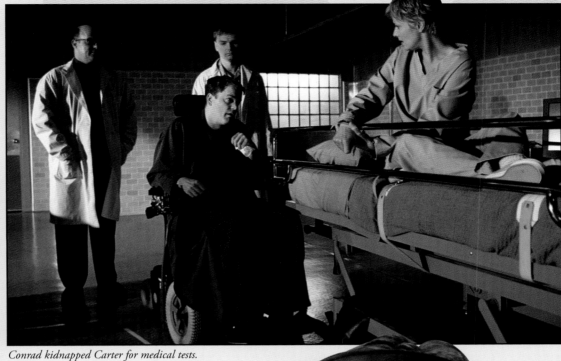

Adrian Conrad became a Goa'uld host.

Conrad kidnapped Carter for medical tests.

COLONEL HARRY MAYBOURNE

Maybourne of the NID had ruthlessly pursued the acquisition of alien technology. Reassigned from the Pentagon to Nellis, he secretly commanded the rogue off-world operation, using the beta stargate from Area 51. When the operation was exposed, he was convicted of treason and faced the death penalty, but O'Neill obtained his temporary release and his cooperation in uncovering illegal NID activities. Maybourne remained a fugitive until he sought O'Neill's help to reach an alien paradise, but both became stranded on the deserted world before being rescued by the Tok'ra.

Maybourne chose to live off-world as King Arkhan.

KING ARKHAN

Maybourne chose to retire off-world, and on a simple planet he discovered Ancient writings that foretold the future. He was honored by the inhabitants as a prophet and accepted the title of King Arkhan the First. After SG-1 saved the planet from conquest by Ares, as the writings had foretold, Maybourne remained among his people, and his wives.

Prisoner S2989

Maybourne became a fugitive.

Russians

RUSSIAN INVOLVEMENT in the Stargate Program began following the loss of the Giza stargate in the crash of Thor's ship. The Russians succeeded in recovering the gate from the Pacific and established their own short lived stargate program in Siberia. By carefully scheduling the connection of a DHD to make the Siberian gate temporarily dominant, the Russians secretly orchestrated several missions, including the search for the Eye of Tiamat on P2X-338 in which all team members died in Marduk's ziggurat on the planet.

The Russian stargate program was shut down after 37 days and seven explored planets.

The Siberian Stargate

UNEASY ALLIANCE

In the aftermath of the disastrous mission to the Water Planet, Russia was reluctant to continue to incur the expense and risk of running its own stargate program. A US-Russian agreement closed down the Siberian stargate and later arranged for its loan to the SGC in exchange for a financial settlement, full disclosure, shared technology, and a permanent Russian presence at the SGC.

Daniel, O'Neill, and Chekov barely averted a Russian-US nuclear crisis.

Russia and the United States were brought to the brink of nuclear war when the Goa'uld infiltrated the Russian and American leadership in an elaborate scheme to eliminate both nations and seize control of the Ancient defense weapon in Antarctica. Through the cooperation of General O'Neill and Colonel Chekov, the world was saved from self annihilation.

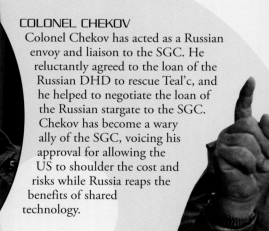

COLONEL CHEKOV

Colonel Chekov has acted as a Russian envoy and liaison to the SGC. He reluctantly agreed to the loan of the Russian DHD to rescue Teal'c, and he helped to negotiate the loan of the Russian stargate to the SGC. Chekov has become a wary ally of the SGC, voicing his approval for allowing the US to shoulder the cost and risks while Russia reaps the benefits of shared technology.

Colonel Chekov was highly suspicious of the deaths of three Russian team members on P2X-338.

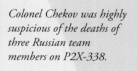

Colonel Chekov and O'Neill

COLONEL ALEXI VASELOV

Alexi Vaselov, a highly decorated Russian officer, had requested a transfer to the SGC. When he was temporarily taken as a host by the disembodied entity of Anubis, however, his body was weakened beyond repair. Vaselov sacrificed his life to save the base by becoming a host to Anubis once more and stepping through the stargate to KS7-535, where he was presumed dead.

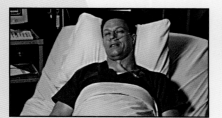

Colonel Vaselov

SVETLANA MARKOV

Dr. Svetlana Markov is a brilliant Russian scientist who helped to establish the Russian stargate program in Siberia. She had been absent from the base when a malfunction prevented the gate from disconnecting from the Water Planet, killing all personnel, and she turned to the SGC for help to determine the cause of the disaster and to shut down the gate.

*Chief Science
Officer, Dr. Markov*

Vaselov spared the SGC by offering Anubis a means of escape.

COLONEL ZUKHOV

Colonel Zukhov commanded the Russian team during the second mission to P2X-338, for which he had secret orders to obtain the Eye of Tiamat. He died in the collapse of Marduk's ziggurat.

MAJOR VALLARIN

On P2X-338, Vallarin was taken as a host by the Goa'uld Marduk, and he was presumed killed in the ruins of the collapsed ziggurat.

LIEUTENANT MARCHENKO

When a booby trap triggered the collapse of corridors within Marduk's ziggurat, Marchenko was crushed to death.

The Russians returned to P2X-338 with SG-1.

LIEUTENANT TOLINEV

Lieutenant Tolinev was bitten by an alien creature from Marduk's tomb, but she was the only member of the Russian team to survive the mission to P2X-338.

MISSIONS

Abydos

THOUSANDS OF YEARS AGO, Ra had brought the Abydonian ancestors from Earth to labor in the naquadah mines in the shadow of his great pyramid. The stargate would reunite the children of Earth when Abydos became the destination of the first stargate mission, and Ra was destroyed. Daniel remained behind on the planet, taking Sha're as his wife, but a year later, when Abydos came under the control of Apophis, O'Neill and Daniel were reunited and the battle with the Goa'uld began.

The Abydonians emulated the Egyptian culture.

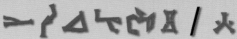

Coordinates: 27-7-15-32-12-30
Point of Origin: (unique)

SG-1 aided the Abydonians in the battle for Abydos.

THE EYE OF RA

Anubis came to Abydos seeking the artifact known as the Eye of Ra, buried deep within Ra's pyramid, and in the battle for Abydos, he used its immense power to create a superweapon which destroyed the planet. However, the Abydonians were spared by Oma Desala, who guided them to ascension, and they began a new journey on a higher plane of existence.

SHA'RE

Sha're met Daniel during the first Abydos mission and became his wife. She was captured by Apophis and made a host to his Goa'uld queen, Amaunet, and she gave birth to Apophis's human child, the Harsesis infant, whom Amaunet sent into hiding. In the search for Sha're and her child, SG-1 encountered Amaunet, who caught Daniel in the grip of her ribbon device. Through the device, Sha're was able to communicate a message of forgiveness and concern for her child, before she was killed by Teal'c to save Daniel's life.

ABYDOS CARTOUCHE

Abydos is relatively close to Earth in the stargate network, making it possible to dial there without compensating for stellar drift. No other stargate addresses were known until Daniel discovered, near Ra's pyramid on Abydos, an ancient map room with a wall of symbols that represented a vast network of stargates. The discovery of the cartouche enabled the SGC to make the necessary calculations for stellar drift that would allow the dialing computer to successfully connect to other planets beyond Abydos. Since then, additional addresses drawn from the library of the Ancients, and not previously known to the Goa'uld, have expanded the SGC's database of known stargates.

The walls of the ancient map room.

Skaara was fatally wounded by a staff weapon.

SKAARA

Skaara befriended O'Neill during the first mission to Abydos and had participated in the defeat of Ra, but he was captured by Apophis and made a host to his Goa'uld son, Klorel. Fleeing Heru'ur, Klorel had crashed on Tollana, and Skaara emerged, pleading for sanctuary. By the decision of the Tollan triad, Skaara was freed from the Goa'uld, and Klorel's symbiote was removed. Skaara returned to his life on Abydos, but he was fatally wounded in the battle against Anubis and was guided toward ascension by Oma Desala.

Skaara became the host to Klorel.

The Tollan detachment device allowed Skaara to speak.

KASUF

Kasuf, the father of Skaara and Sha're, met O'Neill and Daniel during their first mission to Abydos. He welcomed the visitors to his world and offered his daughter, Sha're, in marriage to Daniel. After Sha're gave birth to the infant Harsesis, Kasuf was entrusted with the care of the child, and he sent a message to SG-1 for help when Amaunet stole the child away. Kasuf had led the women and children to safety before Anubis's arrival, but may have joined the Abydonians in ascension as his world was destroyed.

Kasuf remained a friend to Earth.

C HULAK, A HOMEWORLD of the Jaffa, is a forested world with two suns over 2000 light years from Earth. It is the home planet of Teal'c and his family, the destination of the first SG-1 mission beyond Abydos. Chulak had been under the domination of Apophis, and following his defeat by SG-1 the planet endured much unrest as his loyal Jaffa faced opposition from the growing numbers of Rebel Jaffa who followed Bra'tac.

Coordinates: 9-2-23-15-37-20
Point of Origin: 7

JAFFA MASTER

Fiercely independent, a gifted pilot, leader, and teacher, as well as a master warrior, Bra'tac had little patience for humans, however in cooperating with SG-1 he has learned to admire the human spirit, and has become a strong friend and ally of the Tauri. At 133 years old, Bra'tac was nearing an age when he could no longer carry a prim'ta, but since the Ambush of Kresh'taa, regular doses of tretonin have granted him long life free from reliance on a symbiote. Following the conquest of Dakara, Bra'tac accepted a seat on the newly formed High Council to help lead the new Jaffa nation toward a future of freedom.

BRA'TAC

Bra'tac of Chulak is a legendary Master Jaffa warrior, formerly the First Prime of Apophis, for whom he bears the gold serpent tattoo. Bra'tac has long believed that the Goa'uld are false gods and he used his favored position within the court of Apophis to sow the seeds of rebellion. As Teal'c's mentor on Chulak, Bra'tac saw the spark of doubt in his young apprentice, and trained him as his successor, teaching his beliefs of false gods until Teal'c turned against Apophis and joined the Tauri.

Jaffa Armor

Jaffa Staff Weapon

Rebel Leader

RYA'C

When Teal'c joined the Tauri, his young son, Rya'c, had remained behind on Chulak, but Teal'c returned to his homeworld to rescue his son from capture by Apophis and slavery to the Goa'uld. Rya'c trained as an apprentice to Master Bra'tac, but he harbored a deep resentment toward Teal'c for abandoning his family, and their reunion brought an uneasy reconciliation. He grew into a skilled warrior, eventually taking Kar'yn, a young Hak'tyl warrior, as his bride, and joining the Rebel cause at his father's side.

Drey'auc of the Cord'ai Plains.

DREY'AUC

Teal'c's wife, Drey'auc, had been banished with her son following her husband's betrayal of Apophis. Forced to live as an outcast, and believing her husband would not return, she had her marriage removed, and instead married Fro'tak to guarantee a measure of security for herself and her son. However, Fro'tak's betrayal led to his death, and Drey'auc left Chulak with her son, living briefly in the Land of Light before rejoining her people among the camps of the Rebel Jaffa. When her symbiote matured, she was unable to procure another, and Drey'auc died amid the harsh conditions of the Rebel camp.

Teal'c returned to Chulak to rescue his son from Apophis.

Teal'c's reunion with Shan'auc rekindled a romance.

SHAN'AUC

Shan'auc, a Jaffa priestess in the temple of Apophis, came to believe that she could communicate with her symbiote and turn it against the Goa'uld. She came to Earth seeking a means to defeat the Goa'uld, and with the help of the Tok'ra, who hoped to gain counterintelligence, a host was found for the symbiote she carried. However her symbiote, Tanith, had deceived her. Once implanted among the Tok'ra, Tanith's true nature emerged, and he murdered Shan'auc.

Shan'auc of the Red Hills

The Ancients

THE ANCIENTS, ONE OF THE FOUR great races of the Ancient Alliance, were the builders of the stargates. They had evolved millions of years ago from a race of humans that lived long before us, but they were wiped out by a plague that swept across the galaxy. Many learned to ascend to a form of pure energy, but the rest died out. As the Ancient humans vanished following the plague, a device on Dakara was used by the surviving Ancients to begin a second evolution and to recreate life in the Milky Way galaxy.

SG-1 first encountered an Ancient on Kheb.

The Ancients evolved into an ascended form of energy.

ASCENSION

There are many planes of existence between mortal human existence and true enlightenment. The Ancients discovered a means of ascending to a higher plane of existence. In their ascended state they appear as an ethereal glowing light, however they can also remain invisible, or take on a human appearance in a non-corporeal form. They can choose to retake mortal human form, however they require the help of the others to ascend once again. Although ascended Ancients possess extraordinary powers, including the ability to control the forces of nature, ascension does not make one all-knowing or all-powerful. It is merely the beginning of life's journey.

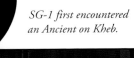

As Daniel Jackson was dying of radiation poisoning, he was guided toward ascension by Oma Desala.

EARTH

Discoveries in Antarctica have shed light on the mysteries of the Ancients and of human evolution on Earth. The preserved body of a woman, later known as Ayiana, near a second stargate in Antarctica suggests the presence of a race of humans on Earth more than 3 million years ago, predating the Antarctic glacier.

Earth was once a homeworld of the Ancients.

TAURI

Legend tells of Tauri (Earth) and its people, where humans evolved to be seeded among the stars.

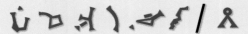

Coordinates: 28-26-5-36-11-29
Point of Origin: 1

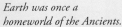

ANCIENT ALLIANCE

There was once an alliance, built over many millennia, of four great races of the galaxy: the Asgard, the Nox, the Furlings, and the Ancients. Today, ancient structures, ruins, and artifacts stretching across the galaxies bear witness to the union that has come to be known as the Ancient Alliance. The Asgard believe that the humans of Earth have already taken the first steps towards becoming the Fifth Race.

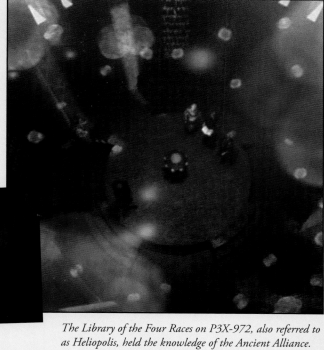

Humans may become the Fifth Race.

The Library of the Four Races on P3X-972, also referred to as Heliopolis, held the knowledge of the Ancient Alliance.

LOST CITY OF ATLANTIS

SG-1 sought the Lost City of the Ancients hoping that it held advanced technologies. Knowledge from the Ancient repository on P3X-439 led SG-1 to Praclarush Taonas where a holographic map at least 30 million years old suggested that the answer lay beneath the ice of Antarctica. In Antarctica, SG-1 found an Ancient outpost with powerful weapons that defeated Anubis and his fleet, but the site was too small to have been the Lost City they sought. However, later research eventually led to the discovery of the Lost City of Atlantis in the Pegasus galaxy.

PRACLARUSH TAONAS

The planet's address glyphs spelled out the name "Praclarush Taonas" where SG-1 found a ZPM.

Coordinates: 35-3-31-29-5-17

P3X-439

SG-1 discovered an Ancient temple ruin and a second repository of knowledge on P3X-439.

P3R-272

SG-1 discovered the first Ancient repository that downloaded knowledge into O'Neill's mind.

VELONA

Orlin had been banished to Velona (P4X-636) for intervening in the planet's development.

KHEB

SG-1 first encountered Oma Desala, an ascended Ancient, on Kheb.

Coordinates: 26-35-6-8-23-14

The Ancients

ALTHOUGH THE ANCIENTS had once been human, those who survive exist in a state of enlightenment as pure energy. The ability to ascend is not limited to the Ancients, however, for if one is pure of spirit, one can choose enlightenment. Those who have ascended, also known as "Others," gain access to the vast knowledge of the Ancients, but they are forbidden from interfering in the natural ascension process of those beneath.

OMA DESALA

Oma Desala, a name meaning "Mother Nature," is an ascended Ancient, an outcast among her kind because she operates beyond the restrictions of the Collective and helps others to ascend, thus breaking the most sacred rule of the Ancients. Long ago, Anubis had deceived Oma Desala to gain the Ancient knowledge. She had helped him to ascend, but realized her horrific mistake too late, and tried in vain to undo it. As punishment, Oma has been forced to watch the consequences of her actions, powerless to interfere as the evil of Anubis gained dominance in the galaxy.

INTERVENTION

Within certain limits, to avoid drawing the wrath of the Others, Oma Desala has continued to guide others toward ascension and to intervene in human existence. SG-1 first encountered her on Kheb, where Amaunet had entrusted her with the Harsesis infant, and as the child grew, Oma taught him to bury the evil Goa'uld knowledge with which he had been born. She returned when Daniel faced death from the effects of radiation poisoning, and she helped to guide him toward ascension and the path of enlightenment.

Oma Desala appeared to Daniel on a higher plane.

ETERNITY

Oma returned once again when Daniel was killed by Replicator Carter, and in a plane of existence between mortality and ascension, Oma and Daniel faced Anubis, in the persona of "Jim." It was Oma's punishment to watch helplessly as Anubis used an Ancient device on Dakara to eliminate all life in the galaxy, but instead she made one final decision to intervene. Locked in eternal struggle, the glowing energies of Oma and Anubis joined as one and vanished.

The name Shifu means "light."

Ayiana was an advanced level of human evolution.

AYIANA

Researchers in Antarctica discovered a young woman buried deep in the glacial ice and were astounded when she miraculously revived. She was given the name Ayiana, which means "eternal bloom," and tests revealed that she was at least 3 million years old, possibly a living Ancient. Ayiana carried a contagion, and although she possessed the remarkable ability to cure the infection as it spread to others, her system was severely weakened with each attempt, and eventually she succumbed to the illness herself.

SHIFU

Shifu, the son of Apophis and Amaunet, is the Harsesis, the forbidden human offspring of two Goa'uld hosts, born with all the knowledge of the Goa'uld. Following his birth on Abydos, he was hidden away on Kheb and raised by Oma Desala, who gave him the name Shifu and taught him to bury the evil in his subconscious. Although he is not an Ancient, Shifu has gained the knowledge of the Ancients and lives as an ascended being among the Others.

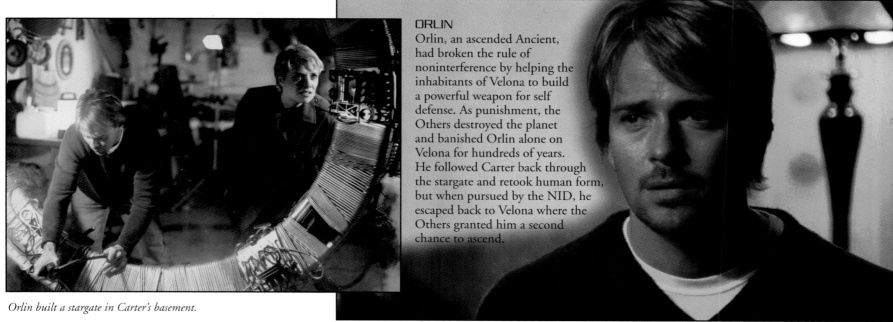

ORLIN

Orlin, an ascended Ancient, had broken the rule of noninterference by helping the inhabitants of Velona to build a powerful weapon for self defense. As punishment, the Others destroyed the planet and banished Orlin alone on Velona for hundreds of years. He followed Carter back through the stargate and retook human form, but when pursued by the NID, he escaped back to Velona where the Others granted him a second chance to ascend.

Orlin built a stargate in Carter's basement.

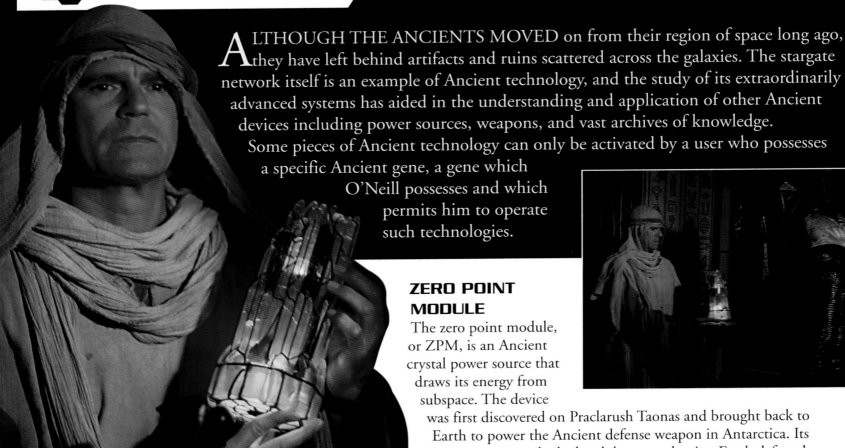

ALTHOUGH THE ANCIENTS MOVED on from their region of space long ago, they have left behind artifacts and ruins scattered across the galaxies. The stargate network itself is an example of Ancient technology, and the study of its extraordinarily advanced systems has aided in the understanding and application of other Ancient devices including power sources, weapons, and vast archives of knowledge.

Some pieces of Ancient technology can only be activated by a user who possesses a specific Ancient gene, a gene which O'Neill possesses and which permits him to operate such technologies.

ZERO POINT MODULE

The zero point module, or ZPM, is an Ancient crystal power source that draws its energy from subspace. The device was first discovered on Praclarush Taonas and brought back to Earth to power the Ancient defense weapon in Antarctica. Its power was severely depleted, however, leaving Earth defenseless until SG-1 journeyed to ancient Egypt to acquire a second ZPM which can now be used to power Earth's defenses and to open a wormhole to the Pegasus galaxy.

SG-1 traveled to 3000 BC to acquire a functioning zero point module.

ANCIENT TABLET
In a sealed chamber in Ra's pyramid on Abydos, SG-1 discovered a stone tablet inscribed in one of the oldest dialects of the Ancients. Daniel and Jonas struggled to decipher the obscure text which told the history of the Ancients and described powerful weapons concealed in a fabled Lost City.

ANCIENT DEFENSE WEAPON
In the Ancient outpost buried beneath the ice of Antarctica, SG-1 discovered a throne-like chair of Ancient design. The chair is powered by a zero point module, and when activated by an individual who possesses the specific Ancient gene, the defense weapon targets and eliminates only enemy forces.

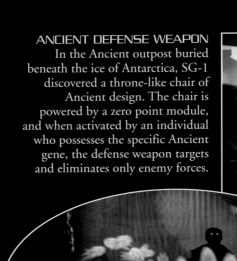

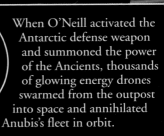

When O'Neill activated the Antarctic defense weapon and summoned the power of the Ancients, thousands of glowing energy drones swarmed from the outpost into space and annihilated Anubis's fleet in orbit.

ANCIENT REPOSITORY

An inscription on P3R-272 reads "Noo Ani Anqueetus" ("We are the Ancients"), and "Hic Qua Videeum" ("The Place of Our Legacy"). A device within a sealed chamber is an archive of all the knowledge of the Ancients, and when O'Neill peered inside, it grasped his head and downloaded an alien database directly into his brain before its power was depleted. Five years later, SG-1 discovered a second Ancient repository on P3X-439. O'Neill once again interfaced with the device, which was destroyed to prevent its capture by Anubis.

The Ancient device grasped O'Neill's head.

ANCIENT SPACECRAFT

A small spacecraft of Ancient design, known by the Atlantis expedition as a "puddle jumper," was designed to be flown through the stargate. Only someone who possesses the Ancient gene can engage and fly the ship.

ANCIENT TIME TRAVEL DEVICE

The spacecraft contained a device which can manifest an energy field that allows the ship to literally fly through time. SG-1 used the device to travel to Egypt in 3000 BC.

Joe Spencer

The stones linked the thoughts of O'Neill and Joe Spencer, a barber from Indiana.

COMMUNICATION STONE

Small rounded black stones with engraved characters function as Ancient long-range communication devices that use a type of psychic connection over great distances between individuals who possess the Ancient gene.

Stones were found on P3R-233 and in Egypt.

The Goa'uld

THE PRIMORDIAL Goa'uld of P3X-888 were snake-like predators that evolved for millions of years in the planet's prehistoric oceans before taking the indigenous aboriginal Unas as hosts. Those who took hosts learned to use the stargate and left the planet, becoming a race of conquerors. The Goa'uld race is violent, arrogant, and parasitic. They are ruthless in battle, and will annihilate that which they cannot enslave or control.

Goa'uld fossils on P3X-888 reveal a species of snake-like predators.

A symbiote queen produces a large egg sac.

Infant Goa'uld are born as snake-like larvae.

New larvae mature in the pouch of a Jaffa for 7 to 8 years.

PHYSIOLOGY

The early Goa'uld species had wing-like appendages allowing them to leap over distances, and naquadah did not become a part of their physical makeup until later in their evolution. Goa'uld larvae are produced by queens who, as symbiotes, will produce large egg sacs and fertilize their own eggs. Goa'uld offspring are born evil, with the genetic memory and the intellect and collective knowledge of their lineage which is passed on voluntarily by the queen who bore them. Symbiotes do not have a gender, but assume a gender once they take a host.

SYMBIOTE AND HOST

Humans have become the preferred host species. A mature symbiote usually enters a host through the back of the neck, attaching itself to the brain stem and taking control of the body. A symbiote grants remarkable healing and regenerative powers and an extended life span, up to 400 years. Once in control, a symbiote can selectively remain dormant or active and choose to exhibit or conceal its characteristic glowing eyes and deep voice. However, while a mature symbiote can take control of the host body at will, the reverse is not true.

Symbiotes have a primal instinct to take a host.

A Goa'uld host can exhibit glowing eyes.

Goa'uld System Lords rule by force and control many hundreds of worlds.

SOCIETY

Goa'uld society is feudal, with thousands of Goa'uld in general, but only dozens at the rank of System Lord. They continuously compete for power, and have been known to engage in sacred ritual cannibalism, thus keeping in check the size of the population and the competition for dominance. Once, their numbers were few, and according to ancient legend, Ra's race was dying, however as the Goa'uld took human hosts and conquered new worlds, their numbers and their power grew.

Ra took the role of sun god and enslaved the people of Earth.

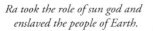

FACT FILE

GOA'ULD DICTIONARY

Arik tree'ac te kek.	We do not surrender, even in death.
Ashrak	Goa'uld assassin, hunter
Bashaak	Jaffa training
Benna! Ya wan ya duru!	Kneel before your masters!
Cal mah	Sanctuary
Chaapa'ai	Stargate
Chel hol	Greeting
Chel nak	Very cool
Chel nok	Good luck
Dal shakka mel!	I die free!
Goach, sha kree, lo Goa'uld.	Tok'ra password response
Hakorr kra terak shree	Banished to oblivion
Hak'tyl	Liberation
Hasshak	Weakling, fodder
Ha'taaka	Slayer of children, poisoner of minds
Hol	Hold, stop
Hol mel	Hold your fire
Joma secu	Challenge of leadership (Follow me)
Kalach	Soul
Kalach shal tek!	Victory or death! (Soul returns home)
Kal'ma	Child
Kek	Kill, dead, weakness (from Unas "keka")
Kel mal tak Tauri!	Destroy the people of Earth!
Kel mar tokeem	Revenge by the wearer of horns
Kel	Where, where is, what, what is
Kel shak	What, what is it, what is going on
Korush'nai	Turn back, radioactive contamination
Kree	Attention, listen, yoo-hoo
Kree no tel, Reenlokia!	The Asgard are approaching!
Kree shac, shel nok.	Bite me
Kree tak?	Is this a trick?
Kree tal shal mak!	Identify yourself!
Kresh'taa	Outcast, banished, untouchable
Lek tol	Signing off
Lok'nel	Ancient Jaffa martial arts
Lo'taur	High ranking human slave
Mak	My identity
Mak lo onak!	Oh my god!
Mak tal shree!	I am a Lord.
Mastaba	Form of Jaffa martial arts
Mekta satak Oz!	My identity is the Great and Powerful Oz!
Mel nok tee!	Evacuate now!
Mok	Your identity

GOA'ULD LANGUAGE

The Goa'uld language, spoken by both the Goa'uld and their Jaffa, is similar to that of ancient Egypt and Abydos, and borrows from the Unas language as well. The Goa'uld word "kek" (kill, dead) evolved from the Unas word "keka." To the Goa'uld, "onac" means "god", whereas to the Unas it means "enemy." Words can have many meanings depending on the context in which they are used. When written, the Goa'uld language is read from right to left.

Mastaba

Tal mak

Korush'nai

Tauri

Mol kek!	Kill them all!
Na'onak	Not a god
Nemeth kree!	You dare touch me!
Nish'ta	Biological brainwashing compound
Niss trah!	I am here!
Nok	Now
Onak	God
Onak sha kree, shel Goa'uld.	What god do you worship? (Tok'ra password)
Orak	Unspeakable, referring to Kull Warriors
Pal tiem shree tal ma.	Our love does not end in death.
Peltac	Bridge of the ship
Prata	Puberty
Prim'ta	Implantation ceremony, larval Goa'uld
Quell shak	Please
Ral tora ke	Good luck
Reenlokia	Asgard
Rin nok!	Silence!
Rin tel nok!	Protect me now!
Ring kol nok	Strategy
Shal kek	Dismissed
Shal met	A toast
Shal tek	Return home, dial home
Shel kek nem ron.	I die free. (Rebel Jaffa password)
Shesh'ta	Jaffa unit of money
Shim'roa	Honeymoon
Shin tel?	What's going on?
Shol'va	Traitor
Sim'ka	Betrothed
Tak	Trick
Tak mal tiak	Greeting
Tal	Wait
Tal mak	A world on which life is now extinct
Tal'ma'te	Affectionate greeting, farewell
Tal pat ryn	Falling star
Tal shak!	Attack!
Tauri	Earth, the people of Earth
Tek'ma'te	Friend, greeting of respect
Tek'ma'tek	Friends well met. We come in peace.
Tel	I, I have
Tel kol	I beg your pardon
Vo'cume	Holographic projector
Ya duru arik kek onac.	I honor him who would kill his god.
Zatarc	Programmed assassin

Chappa'ai

Shol'va

Goa'uld Pantheon

The Goa'uld are driven to conquer, to claim worlds as their own and rule as gods. Thousands of years ago, Ra had established a power base on Earth, using the religion of the ancient Egyptians to enslave them. As Goa'uld power and influence expanded, many cultures became increasingly linked to the race of conquerors who sought to exploit Earth's religions.

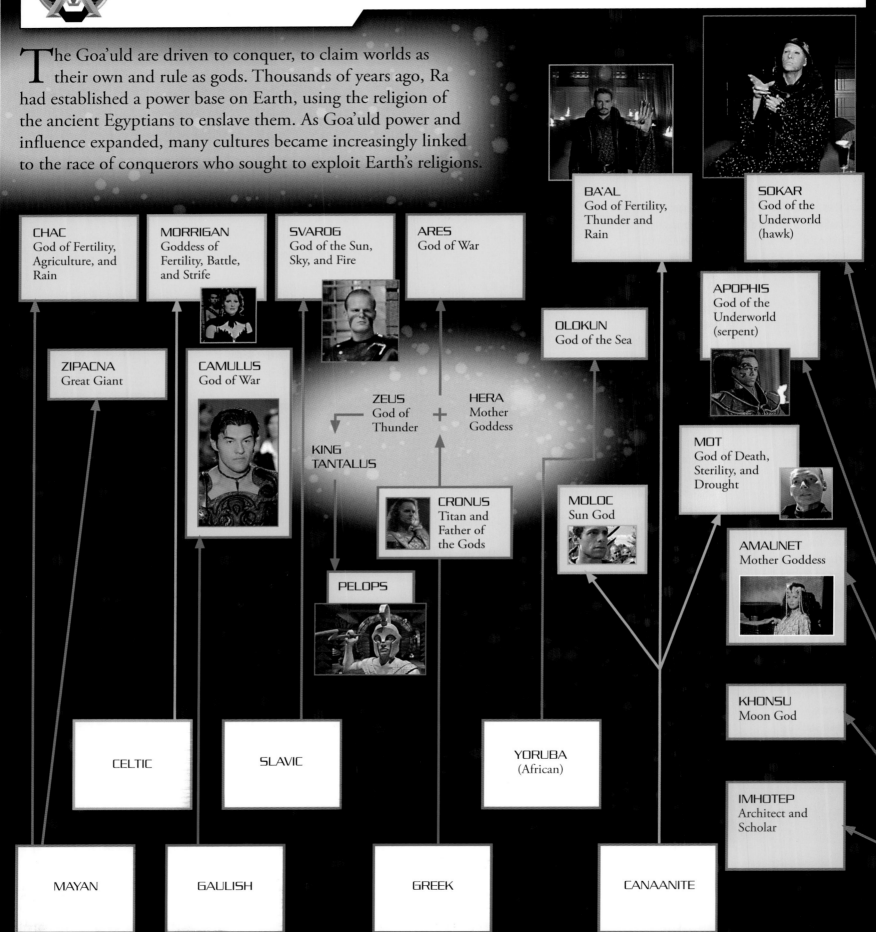

BA'AL
God of Fertility, Thunder and Rain

SOKAR
God of the Underworld (hawk)

CHAC
God of Fertility, Agriculture, and Rain

MORRIGAN
Goddess of Fertility, Battle, and Strife

SVAROG
God of the Sun, Sky, and Fire

ARES
God of War

APOPHIS
God of the Underworld (serpent)

OLOKUN
God of the Sea

ZIPACNA
Great Giant

CAMULUS
God of War

ZEUS
God of Thunder

HERA
Mother Goddess

KING TANTALUS

CRONUS
Titan and Father of the Gods

MOLOC
Sun God

MOT
God of Death, Sterility, and Drought

AMAUNET
Mother Goddess

PELOPS

KHONSU
Moon God

IMHOTEP
Architect and Scholar

CELTIC

SLAVIC

YORUBA
(African)

MAYAN

GAULISH

GREEK

CANAANITE

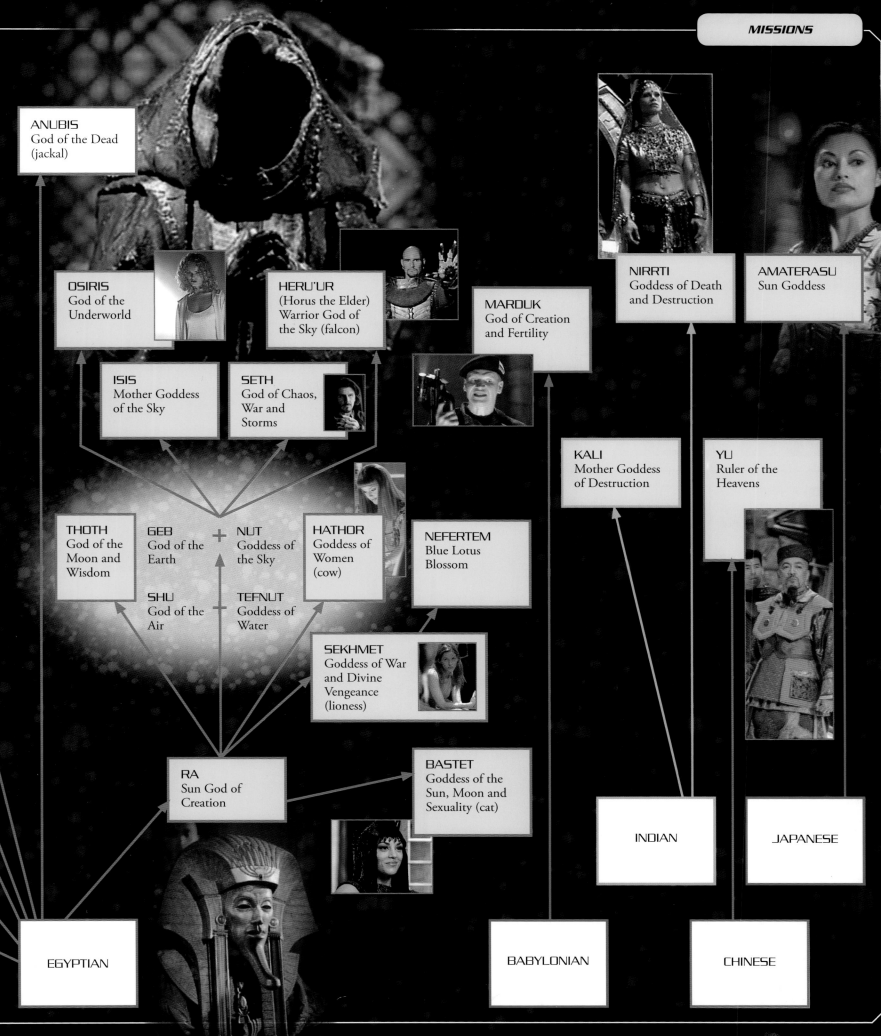

ANUBIS
God of the Dead
(jackal)

OSIRIS
God of the
Underworld

HERU'UR
(Horus the Elder)
Warrior God of
the Sky (falcon)

MARDUK
God of Creation
and Fertility

NIRRTI
Goddess of Death
and Destruction

AMATERASU
Sun Goddess

ISIS
Mother Goddess
of the Sky

SETH
God of Chaos,
War and
Storms

THOTH
God of the
Moon and
Wisdom

GEB
God of the
Earth

NUT
Goddess of
the Sky

HATHOR
Goddess of
Women
(cow)

NEFERTEM
Blue Lotus
Blossom

KALI
Mother Goddess
of Destruction

YU
Ruler of the
Heavens

SHU
God of the
Air

TEFNUT
Goddess of
Water

SEKHMET
Goddess of War
and Divine
Vengeance
(lioness)

RA
Sun God of
Creation

BASTET
Goddess of the
Sun, Moon and
Sexuality (cat)

INDIAN

JAPANESE

EGYPTIAN

BABYLONIAN

CHINESE

Anubis

LEGEND TELLS THAT the temple at Dakara is the place where Anubis rose from the dead. An ancient and powerful Goa'uld, Anubis had long ago been banished by the System Lords, never to be allowed to return, for crimes unspeakable even to the Goa'uld. The System Lords had tried to murder him, and believed him to be dead for at least a thousand years. However, Anubis had not died. He had discovered the mystery of ascension.

Anubis existed in a partially ascended plane.

FACT FILE

ASTEROID
Anubis sent an artificial asteroid composed of naquadah on a collision course with Earth to make Earth's destruction appear as a natural disaster.

ANCIENT WEAPON

Anubis used Ancient technology to create a weapon which used one stargate to overpower another, and he directed it against Earth's stargate.

EYE OF RA
Anubis collected six artifacts including the Eyes of Apophis, Osiris, Tiamat, and Ra. Used in combination, their power is increased tenfold.

SUPERWEAPON
Anubis used the power of the Eyes to create a superweapon with which he destroyed Abydos and defeated the System Lords.

RISE OF ANUBIS
Anubis had journeyed to Kheb where he deceived Oma Desala and learned the path to a higher plane of existence. In doing so, he acquired access to the knowledge of the Ancients. The Others cast him out, but they did not send him back completely. Instead, he remained as a form of energy, existing in a state between mortal existence and ascension, and the Others used their collective powers to prevent him from using the Ancient knowledge.

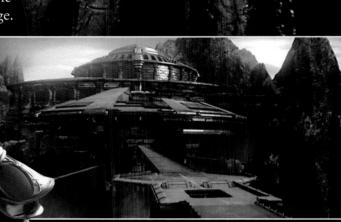

GALACTIC DOMINATION
Using the advanced technologies of the Ancients and the Asgard, Anubis decimated the forces of the System Lords, and he rebuilt his army of warriors, including the Ninja Jaffa who bore his tattoo of the jackal. Although his fleet was defeated at Kelowna, Anubis fled to Tartarus where he raised a new army of Kull Warriors.

Kull Warriors are synthetically created Goa'uld drone soldiers.

KULL WARRIORS
Anubis used knowledge of Egeria and Ancient reanimation technology to give rise to an army of Kull Warriors, Goa'uld creatures without genetic memory which have been implanted into a synthetically created host body and fused into an impenetrable armor. Far superior to the Jaffa, Kull Warriors make the perfect foot soldier: deadly, fearless, and unquestioningly loyal.

Tartarus Coordinates: 33-28-23-26-16-31

O'Neill activated the Ancient defense weapon.

BATTLE OF ANTARCTICA

With his dominance assured, Anubis gathered the full force of his fleet and sent more than 30 motherships into Earth's orbit. Over 2000 American servicemen and women were killed in the attack that would later be explained to the public as a meteor shower. As the battle raged, O'Neill drew upon the knowledge of the Ancients and activated the Ancient defense drones which swarmed into orbit and annihilated Anubis and his fleet in a devastating battle over Antarctica. Anubis was presumed destroyed, creating an unstable vacuum which Ba'al stepped in to fill.

The fate of Earth was determined in the battle above Antarctica.

Although badly disfigured, Anubis escaped from KS7-535.

ANUBIS RETURNS

Anubis had not been eliminated in Antarctica. His disembodied essence took hosts on Earth, eventually inhabiting Colonel Alexi Vaselov, who had been sent on assignment to the SGC. Unable to use his Ancient powers without drawing the wrath of the Others, Anubis sought a way to escape through the stargate, however his escape was thwarted when the dialing sequence was altered to KS7-535, a barren ice planet.

Anubis took Alexi Vaselov as a host to escape from Earth.

Anubis was sent to the frozen world of KS7-535.

DAKARA

Anubis intended to use an Ancient device on Dakara to destroy all life in the galaxy. On a plane of existence between mortality and ascension, he encountered Oma Desala and Daniel, both powerless to kill him. However, Oma prevented the destruction of the galaxy by choosing at last to intervene and forcing Anubis to remain locked in battle with her for all eternity.

Anubis assumed the persona of "Jim."

Anubis's Ancient knowledge led him to Dakara.

System Lords

THE GOA'ULD WEAKNESS is their feudal nature. Although they will reluctantly unite to defend against outside threats, they battle among themselves for supreme domination, and the balance of power continually shifts as System Lords rise to power and are eliminated by their rivals. The greatest danger has been the threat of a single Goa'uld rising to dominant power and overtaking the System Lord collective.

HERU'UR
Heru'ur, or Horus the Elder, son of Ra and Hathor, was a powerful and much feared conqueror, guarded by an army of Horus Guards and Jaffa who bore his symbol of a falcon. When Heru'ur and Apophis had grown to control the two largest armies of the Goa'uld, Apophis lured Heru'ur to a meeting in the minefield of the Tobin System on the pretext of discussing an alliance, but with the intention of destroying Heru'ur with his cloaked fleet. His deception succeeded, Heru'ur was destroyed, and his forces were absorbed into the forces of Apophis.

Heru'ur conquered Tagrea, Juna, and Cimmeria.

SYSTEM LORDS
The System Lords are the few dozen of the ruling class in the Goa'uld hierarchy. Usually they assume the persona of a god and rule many worlds by force through their armies of elite Jaffa warriors. They view Earth as an enemy and have sought to destroy it, however they fear the Asgard, who have used their power to protect certain planets from conquest. Through the intervention of Thor, the System Lords permitted the inclusion of Earth under the Protected Planets Treaty.

At the summit of System Lords in the Hassara System, the reemergence of Anubis threatened the balance of power.

APOPHIS
Apophis, the Egyptian serpent god, ruled the night, rival to his brother Ra who ruled the day. Both Bra'tac and Teal'c had served as his First Prime, commanding his elite army of Serpent Guards. Apophis had conquered many worlds including Pangar, Cartago, Abydos, and Chulak, and by absorbing the forces of his rivals, Heru'ur and Sokar, Apophis had once commanded the largest of the Goa'uld armies. However, he was killed when his mothership was infiltrated by Replicators.

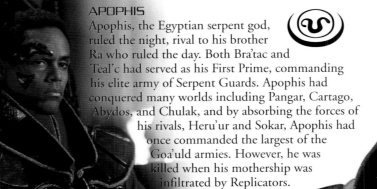

Apophis's host was a scribe from the Temple of Amon at Karnak.

RA

Ra, the brother and rival of Apophis, had taken a young Egyptian boy as a host and used the religion of the ancient Egyptians to rule Earth as their sun god. In 2995 BC, the Egyptians rebelled, and the stargate at Giza was buried. Ra was forced to abandon Earth, and he established a new homeworld on Abydos. Five thousand years after leaving Earth, Ra was killed by O'Neill during the first mission to Abydos when a nuclear warhead was released on his mothership in orbit above the planet.

Ra was attended by Horus Guards and Jaffa bearing his tattoo of the Eye of Ra.

A chemical organism in her breath gave Hathor power over men.

HATHOR

The Egyptian goddess of fertility, inebriety, and music (or "sex, drugs, and rock and roll" according to O'Neill) was both the daughter and wife of Ra. As a "Queen of the Gods," Hathor produced the larval Goa'uld. She had been imprisoned in stasis for almost 2000 years in a sarcophagus in the Mayan Temple of the Inscriptions in Palenque, Mexico, but when freed, she used her power over men to escape from Earth and rebuild her army. At her offworld base, she was defeated by O'Neill, thrown into a cryogenic vat, and presumed killed when the base was destroyed.

SOKAR

Sokar was a Goa'uld of ancient times, the original god of death. He had transformed Netu, the moon orbiting his homeworld of Delmak, with rivers of fire to match the description of hell, and he made it a prison. Although once banished by Cronus, he slowly regained his powerbase, and he captured and imprisoned Apophis on Netu, repeatedly torturing him and reviving him from death. Jacob, Martouf, and SG-1 also became his prisoners on Netu, however Sokar was killed when SG-1 escaped from the prison moon and destroyed both Netu and Sokar's mothership in orbit above it.

System Lords

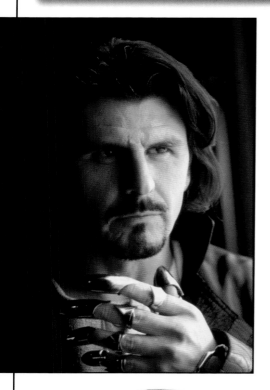

W ITH THE DEATHS of Ra, Hathor, Heru'ur, Sokar, and Apophis at the hands of SG-1, the old order had fallen. The resultant void created a power vacuum and heralded a new order which Anubis threatened to exploit. As Anubis rose to a position of supreme domination, Yu and Ba'al led the collective forces of the System Lords against him. Following the battle of Antarctica, Ba'al gained control of Anubis's army, but the System Lords were forced to unite to face their greatest enemy—the Replicators.

Nirrti had traded Cassandra's life for her freedom.

SETH

Seth, the Egyptian god of chaos, was the embodiment of evil. Also known as Setesh, he was represented by an animal that was either fictitious or extinct, the source of many jokes among the Jaffa. Believed to have been killed in ancient Egypt, Seth had been hiding out on Earth as the leader of various religious cults. As Seth Fargough, he led a cult of about 50 followers in a compound outside Seattle. SG-1 led the mission to find Seth, during which Carter used a ribbon device to kill him.

NIRRTI

Nirrti was a destructive goddess of darkness in Hindu reference. From her underground laboratory, she had conducted experiments on the children of Hanka, hoping to create "hok'tar," an advanced human host. To hide her experiments she wiped out the entire population of Hanka, leaving Cassandra as the planet's only survivor. On P3X-367 she used a DNA resequencer to continue her genetic experiments until Wodan, one of the planet's inhabitants, snapped her neck using the power of telekinesis her experiments had granted him.

Osiris's consort, Isis, perished in stasis.

OSIRIS

Osiris and his consort Isis were "banished to oblivion" by Seth, who placed their symbiotes in stasis in canopic jars. When the artifacts were recovered, Osiris escaped and took a female host in the body of Sarah Gardner, a former associate of Daniel's. Osiris joined forces with Anubis, but she was captured on Earth by SG-1, and the symbiote was successfully removed from the host.

CRONUS

Cronus, one of the twelve Greek Titans, was the god of fate and one of the most influential of the System Lords. Teal'c's father, Ronac, had once served as his First Prime until he was killed by Cronus for failure in battle. With Nirrti and Yu, Cronus participated in the negotiations to include Earth in the Protected Planets Treaty. On Juna, Cronus encountered SG-1 and their synthetic duplicates, and as he confronted Teal'c in battle, he was killed by Teal'c's duplicate, shot in the back by a staff weapon.

Cronus's Jaffa wore the symbol of ram's horns.

BA'AL

Ba'al, a ruthless and vindictive Goa'uld, had allied himself with Anubis, but he eventually changed loyalties and led the combined forces of the United Alliance of System Lords against him. Following Anubis's defeat, Ba'al stood poised to dominate the galaxy, however with the arrival of the Replicators, he allied himself with SG-1 against their common enemy, and he assisted Carter and Jacob in modifying the Ancient weapon of Dakara which defeated the Replicators.

Ba'al is one of the few System Lords to survive the invasion of the Replicators.

Lord Yu had founded the first recorded dynasty of China.

YU

Yu the Great, or Lord Yu Huang Shang-ti, the Jade Emperor, was the oldest of the System Lords and had reigned for countless centuries. Once powerful and feared, he had grown increasingly paranoid and confused with age. He had led the collective forces of the System Lords against Anubis, but with Yu's mental competence failing, Ba'al took command in his place and became a bitter adversary. With the arrival of the Replicators, Yu was killed by Replicator Carter, stabbed in the heart by her bladed weapon.

中

Yu could no longer take a new host or benefit from the sarcophagus.

Goa'uld Technology

THE GOA'ULD ARE CAPABLE of interstellar travel and possess several types of transport and fighter craft. Goa'uld ships rely on crystal technology and most are protected by defensive shields. The largest of the vessels, the ha'tak motherships, often carry fleets of the smaller death gliders. Despite their size, ha'tak ships are capable of landing, and pyramid structures on planets such as Earth or Abydos were built as landing pedestals for Goa'uld motherships.

Hyperspace travel

Goa'uld mothership

Ha'tak use a pyramid design

HA'TAK
The Goa'uld ha'tak class vessel, or pyramid ship, is an attack vessel, also referred to as a mothership. It is capable of hyperspace travel and is heavily armed and shielded, but most ha'tak ships do not use cloaking technology. Motherships are large enough to carry thousands of warriors and to launch a legion of death gliders. They are also able to destroy a planet from space. The Goa'uld have hundreds of these vessels, and System Lords operate entire fleets. Typically a Goa'uld flagship is several times the size of a ha'tak class ship.

Alkesh can carry vast armies.

ALKESH
The alkesh is a Goa'uld mid-range bomber. It is capable of hyperspace travel and is typically equipped with a ring transporter and cloaking capabilities. Able to attack a Goa'uld mothership because of its speed and maneuverability, the alkesh is less maneuverable than a death glider, but superior in size and armaments. Often used by the Goa'uld for aerial attacks, the alkesh can also carry vast armies for ground assaults.

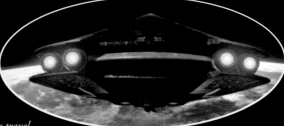

Alkesh are capable of hyperspace travel.

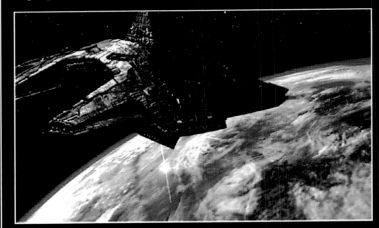

A ha'tak is capable of destroying a planet from orbit.

TELTAC
A teltac is a cargo ship, sometimes referred to as a scout ship, often used by the Goa'uld and the Tok'ra. Capable of achieving hyperspace, most are equipped with cloaking technology, transport rings, and descent pods. Teltacs are maneuverable because of their size, however they are not armed since they are used primarily as transport vessels. Although the SGC has not accumulated its own fleet of teltac vessels, SG-1 has frequently used cargo ships in joint missions with the Tok'ra or Rebel Jaffa, and both Teal'c and O'Neill, as well as Bra'tac and Jacob, are experienced teltac pilots.

Teltacs are maneuverable but unarmed.

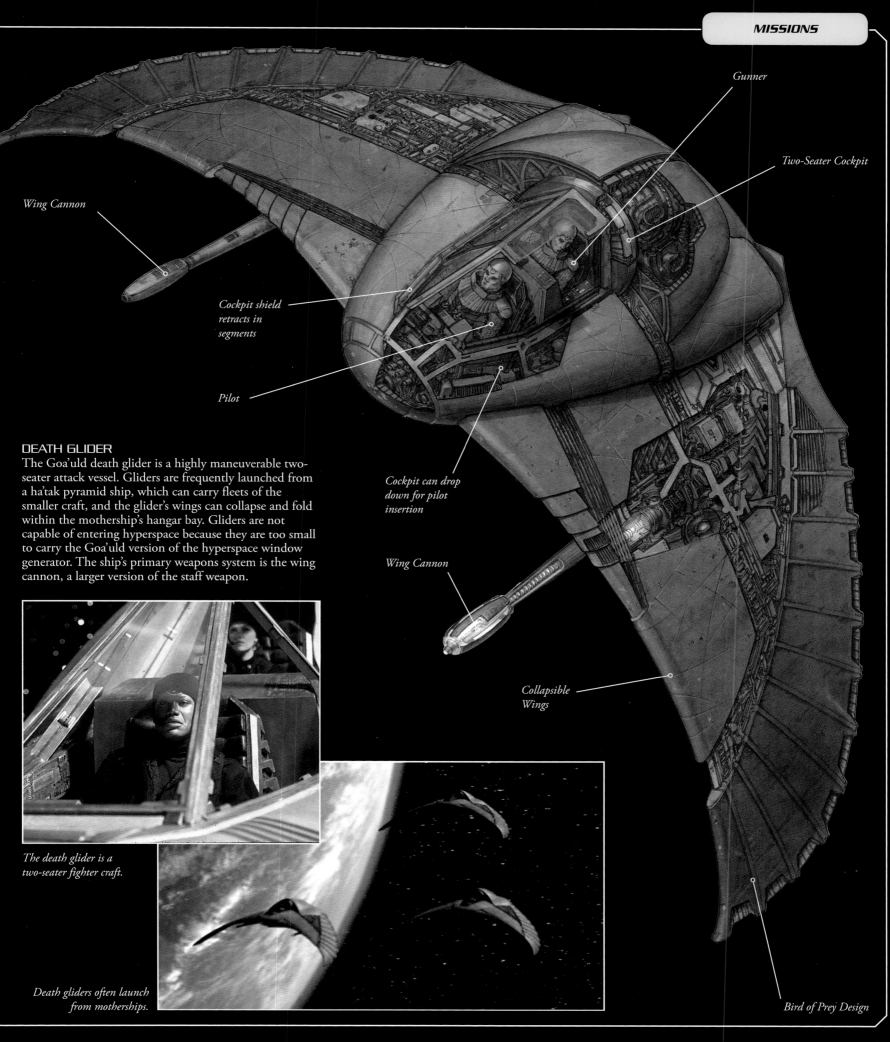

Gunner

Two-Seater Cockpit

Wing Cannon

Cockpit shield retracts in segments

Pilot

DEATH GLIDER

The Goa'uld death glider is a highly maneuverable two-seater attack vessel. Gliders are frequently launched from a ha'tak pyramid ship, which can carry fleets of the smaller craft, and the glider's wings can collapse and fold within the mothership's hangar bay. Gliders are not capable of entering hyperspace because they are too small to carry the Goa'uld version of the hyperspace window generator. The ship's primary weapons system is the wing cannon, a larger version of the staff weapon.

Cockpit can drop down for pilot insertion

Wing Cannon

Collapsible Wings

The death glider is a two-seater fighter craft.

Death gliders often launch from motherships.

Bird of Prey Design

Goa'uld Technology

The Goa'uld are scavengers who have stolen most of their technology from other races. The SGC has acquired several key pieces of Goa'uld technology, however others, such as the ribbon device, require the presence of naquadah in the blood of the user and can only be operated by one who has been a Goa'uld host.

STAFF CANNON
The staff cannon is a larger, more powerful version of a staff weapon and is often used in stationary battle emplacements.

The staff cannon is mounted on a base.

ZAT'NIK'TEL
The zat'nik'tel, or "zat gun," is a hand weapon which delivers an electrical charge. One shot disables, two shots within seconds will kill, and three shots will cause a subject to vanish completely. The zat'nik'tel does not require the presence of naquadah in the blood for operation, making it a valuable technological asset for Earth. Since the second year of the SGC, zat guns have been used by SG teams during off-world missions.

Retracted position

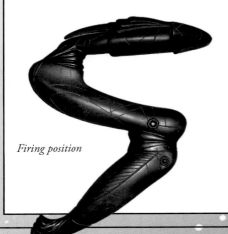

Firing position

Carter and Teal'c carry a zat'nik'tel sidearm.

Teal'c is skilled in the use of the staff weapon.

STAFF WEAPON
The staff weapon is the preferred weapon of Jaffa warriors. It uses a liquid naquadah power source and fires an energy plasma blast, the power of which may vary depending on factors such as the time allowed for recycling between shots. Although it does not rely on naquadah in the blood, the staff weapon has not been adopted for use by the SGC. It is a weapon of great power and endurance, but less accurate than Earth weapons such as the P-90.

Jaffa staff weapon

RIBBON DEVICE

The ribbon device, or hand device, channels energy through amplification crystals, using thought control amplified with emotion. The device relies on the presence of naquadah in the blood and can only be used by those who have been hosts. It is frequently integrated into the Goa'uld wrist device, which incorporates the remote control for various Goa'uld technologies such as the personal force field or ring transporter. Worn on the left hand, the ribbon device can subdue, stun, deflect, paralyze, torture, or kill.

The ribbon device fits over the fingertips.

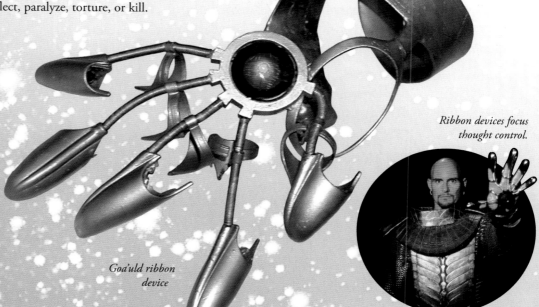

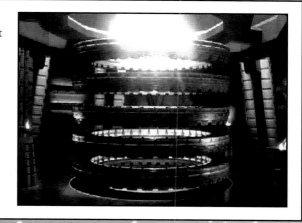

Ribbon devices focus thought control.

Small devices can be used for personal communication.

Goa'uld ribbon device

COMMUNICATION DEVICE

The long-range visual communication device is used for communicating over distances. It projects both a visual and audio signal within a spherical device, similar in its function to a television. The device comes in a variety of sizes from very large to palm-sized, and may be used for public addresses as well as private personal communications. It does not require the presence of naquadah, and was among the technologies acquired by the rogue NID.

Large devices can be used for public broadcast.

RING TRANSPORTER

Transport rings, like stargates, are Ancient crystal technology stolen by the Goa'uld. They transmit a matter stream over short distances, for example between a planet and a ship in orbit. When activated, a set of five rings appears and a beam of light dematerializes and transports any matter within them. At distances within approximately five meters, the rings can function independently, however they are designed to operate in pairs, each ring mechanism detecting other rings to complete a connection.

SARCOPHAGUS

The sarcophagus is capable of curing diseases, healing injuries, reviving the dead, and extending life by thousands of years. The first sarcophagus was created by the Goa'uld Telchak who attempted to harness the life-giving energy of the Ancient reanimation device. In modifying its technology, however, Telchak was unable to eliminate all its negative side effects. Repeated use causes a euphoric narcotic effect, significant psychological changes, and acute physical addiction. The Tok'ra do not use the sarcophagus, believing it takes away one's soul.

The Jaffa

THE WARRIOR JAFFA CLASS has been the foundation of Goa'uld power. The Jaffa ancestors were descendants of the Tauri who were bred to have an abdominal pouch in which a larval Goa'uld, or symbiote, was carried to maturity. When a young child comes of age, he is called to the religious life of his god, and in the prim'ta ritual, or ceremony of implantation, he receives his first Goa'uld symbiote and becomes a true Jaffa. The planet Dakara, the site of the first prim'ta ritual, is sacred to all Jaffa, the very cradle of their existence that has bonded them in servitude to the Goa'uld.

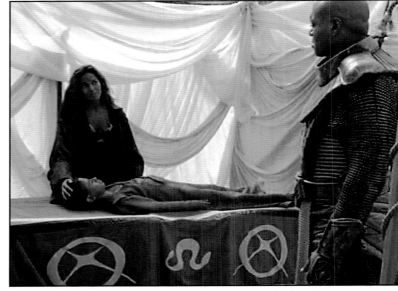

Rya'c is prepared for the prim'ta ceremony.

PHYSIOLOGY

The symbiote functions as the Jaffa's immune system, granting perfect health and long life, and removal of a symbiote would result in death within hours. The daily ritual of kelno'reem, or deep meditation, allows the symbiote to maintain the balance of health. When a symbiote reaches maturity in seven to eight years, it must then take a host, and the Jaffa must take a new symbiote, extending his life span to nearly 140 years, the approximate age when a symbiote would reject the host.

The abdominal pouch is similar to that of a marsupial.

SOCIETY

Highly trained Jaffa warriors serve as the army of the Goa'uld, an army protected by the restorative powers of the Goa'uld larvae they carry. Through intense bashaak training, a young Jaffa becomes a warrior, and Jaffa children are born with the knowledge that weakness will not be tolerated. Each Jaffa bears a forehead tattoo indicating the Goa'uld he serves, a tattoo of pure gold representing the rank of First Prime.

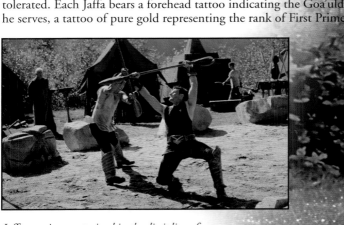

Jaffa warriors are trained in the discipline of mastaba, a form of martial arts.

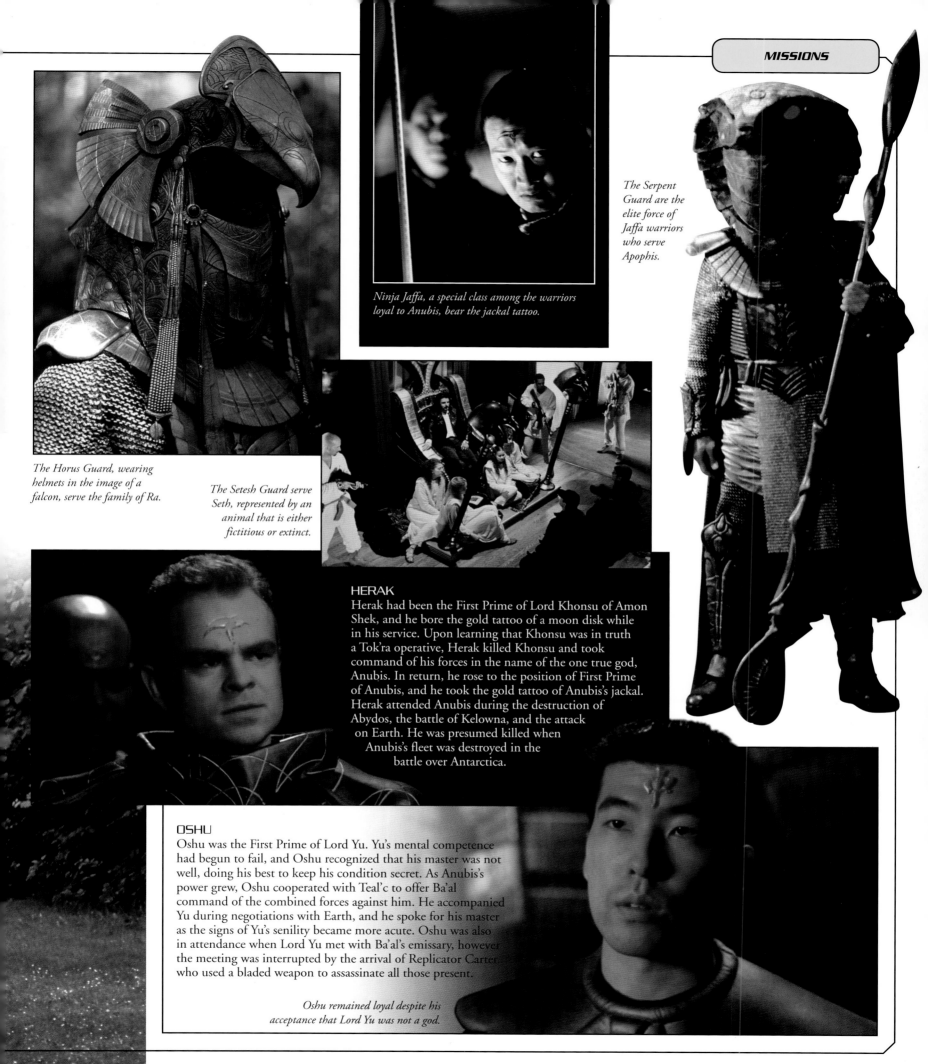

The Serpent Guard are the elite force of Jaffa warriors who serve Apophis.

Ninja Jaffa, a special class among the warriors loyal to Anubis, bear the jackal tattoo.

The Horus Guard, wearing helmets in the image of a falcon, serve the family of Ra.

The Setesh Guard serve Seth, represented by an animal that is either fictitious or extinct.

HERAK

Herak had been the First Prime of Lord Khonsu of Amon Shek, and he bore the gold tattoo of a moon disk while in his service. Upon learning that Khonsu was in truth a Tok'ra operative, Herak killed Khonsu and took command of his forces in the name of the one true god, Anubis. In return, he rose to the position of First Prime of Anubis, and he took the gold tattoo of Anubis's jackal. Herak attended Anubis during the destruction of Abydos, the battle of Kelowna, and the attack on Earth. He was presumed killed when Anubis's fleet was destroyed in the battle over Antarctica.

OSHU

Oshu was the First Prime of Lord Yu. Yu's mental competence had begun to fail, and Oshu recognized that his master was not well, doing his best to keep his condition secret. As Anubis's power grew, Oshu cooperated with Teal'c to offer Ba'al command of the combined forces against him. He accompanied Yu during negotiations with Earth, and he spoke for his master as the signs of Yu's senility became more acute. Oshu was also in attendance when Lord Yu met with Ba'al's emissary, however the meeting was interrupted by the arrival of Replicator Carter, who used a bladed weapon to assassinate all those present.

Oshu remained loyal despite his acceptance that Lord Yu was not a god.

Rebel Jaffa

ALTHOUGH THE JAFFA had been indoctrinated from childhood to worship the Goa'uld, the teachings of Bra'tac and others had led to the growing belief that the Goa'uld are false gods. Despite infighting among Jaffa who had been enemies for centuries, a Jaffa Rebellion gained momentum, and with the eventual victory at Dakara, those who survived were united as never before. Upon the ruins of Dakara would be built a new nation of free Jaffa.

Hak'tyl warriors bear a similarity to the Amazons of Greek mythology.

K'TANO

K'tano claimed that he was once the First Prime of Imhotep, and that he had killed his lord as a false god. A charismatic leader who demanded blind faith from his followers, K'tano gathered a diverse army of Jaffa at a secret base on Cal Mah, and both Teal'c and Bra'tac offered him support as the future hope of the Jaffa Rebellion. In reality, however, K'tano was the false identity of Imhotep himself, whose true intention was to wrest power from the System Lords. When his deception was exposed, he was killed by Teal'c in the rite of joma secu.

Imhotep, a minor Goa'uld, took the persona of K'tano, his former First Prime, with the intention of overthrowing the System Lords.

HAK'TYL

The Hak'tyl, whose name means "liberation," are the female Jaffa warriors of Moloc's domain. Thirty years ago, Moloc decreed that all female children were to be sacrificed in the ceremony of fire. However, under the leadership of Ishta, priestesses and female warriors secretly took the female infants away to safety and raised an army. The Hak'tyl are strong allies of the SGC and the Rebel Jaffa.

RAK'NOR

Delnor of Chulak had followed Bra'tac's rebellion and sought to give his son, Rak'nor, freedom from false gods by searing the serpent tattoo from Rak'nor's forehead. However, when his family was killed by Apophis, Rak'nor saved himself by declaring his loyalty to Apophis as his god. He betrayed Teal'c on Chulak and turned him over to Heru'ur, to be tortured by Terok, however, after witnessing Teal'c's conviction in the face of torture, Rak'nor had a change of heart. He rescued Teal'c and helped him to escape, eventually espousing Teal'c's belief in false gods, and joining the Jaffa Rebellion.

Ishta had once enjoyed a position of privilege as a temple high priestess.

ISHTA

Ishta, the proud and determined leader of the Hak'tyl, abandoned her life as a temple priestess to lead an army of female warriors. Ishta proposed an alliance with the Tauri, and reluctantly came to accept tretonin as a means of freedom for her people. Determined to see the elimination of Moloc, Ishta allied herself with the SGC and the Rebel Jaffa, and she has remained a close friend of Teal'c, with whom a romantic relationship has begun.

ARON

Aron, one of the Rebel Jaffa within Moloc's ranks, had allied himself with Ishta and the Hak'tyl. When a summit of Rebel leaders was ambushed, Ishta and Teal'c suspected that Aron could have been a traitor, but he proved his loyalty when he rescued Teal'c from capture and assisted in defeating Moloc by manually directing the SGC's laser guided missiles to their target. Aron joined Bra'tac, Teal'c, and Tolok in the battle against Ba'al's forces to capture the temple at Dakara, and following the victory at Dakara, he remained to help build the new nation of free Jaffa.

Following Moloc's death, Aron joined the Rebel army.

Missions: Year 1

THROUGH THE EVENT horizon lay unimagined wonders and a galaxy populated by the ancient peoples of Earth. SG-1's earliest missions sought to rescue Sha're and Skaara from Apophis and to recover technologies to defend Earth from the Goa'uld, but their explorations uncovered so much more. Although still very "young," SG-1 made first contact with the Nox and the Asgard, and the discovery at Heliopolis offered a first glimpse into the secrets of the universe.

A contagious virus was brought back to Earth.

P3X-562

The blue quartz crystals native to P3X-562 are living beings. Known as Unity, the non-biological lifeforms are capable of emulating and recreating other lifeforms, but few of the Unity remain since their destruction by the Goa'uld long ago. The crystals are peaceful, and when O'Neill was accidentally injured by the energy from one of them, it tried to heal him. Not understanding the concept of death, the crystal duplicated O'Neill and his son Charlie, hoping to heal O'Neill's greatest pain, the loss of his son.

Coordinates: 3-28-9-35-24-15
Point of Origin: 14

LAND OF LIGHT

The Land of Light is a forested world whose unique rotation causes one half of the planet to be perpetually light, and the other always in darkness. Those inhabiting the dark side exhibited physical and behavioral characteristics similar to primitive man and were believed to have been touched by evil. However, as the same symptoms spread among SGC personnel, it was determined that a highly contagious histaminolytic virus was responsible. Powerful antihistamines provided a cure, and the inhabitants of the Land of Light have become friends and allies of Earth.

THE NOX

The misty forested world of P3X-774 is home to the Nox, a gentle race who appeared innocent and helpless. In fact, the Nox are a highly advanced people, once members of the Ancient Alliance, who possess huge floating cities and who have mastered the power to manipulate invisibility and to raise the dead. The Nox are peaceful and defend themselves through illusion and mastery of the mind. Following SG-1's departure, they intended to bury their stargate, making return impossible. The Nox declined SG-1's assistance, but "the very young do not always do what they're told."

ARGOS

On a world of beauty, the Argosians lived blissful lives, unaware that their ancestors had been brought to Argos by the Goa'uld Pelops as part of an experiment in human physiology and evolution. A nano-virus designed to accelerate normal aging had shortened the lifespan of the Argosians to approximately one hundred days. Through physical contact, the virus was unwittingly passed on to O'Neill, who aged at an alarming rate, until SG-1 succeeded in reversing the experiment, granting the population long healthy lives.

O'Neill aged to the equivalent of 90 years in a few days.

The Argosians joyously celebrated one hundred blissful days.

CIMMERIA

The Cimmerians honored the ways of Thor, who had brought their ancestors from Earth and who protected their world from the Goa'uld by a device known as Thor's Hammer. However, Teal'c became trapped within the maze of Thor's Hammer, and SG-1 was forced to destroy the device to free him, leaving Cimmeria vulnerable. When Heru'ur invaded the planet, SG-1 sought the aid of Thor, whose forces would vanquish the Goa'uld. Through the Hall of Thor's Might, SG-1 first encountered the Asgard race, and Thor revealed himself in his true form.

HELIOPOLIS

In 1945, Ernest Littlefield had stepped through the stargate and was lost. On P3X-972, SG-1 found Ernest in the crumbling ruins where he had lived alone for 50 years, but the ancient castle held a greater mystery, a device Ernest had called "Heliopolis," which acted as a Rosetta Stone to a vast library of knowledge of four great races. During a violent storm, the castle was destroyed, and now only Ernest's and Daniel's notes remain.

Catherine Langford, who had been Ernest's fiancée, joined SG-1's mission to P3X-972.

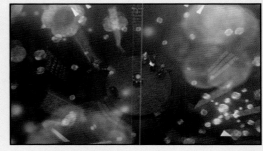

The key to our existence could be "meaning of life stuff."

Missions: Year 1-2

FOR THOUSANDS of years, Earth had been abandoned by the Goa'uld. Since learning the secrets of the stargate, however, the Tauri had ventured beyond their world, making Earth a target for conquest. As SG-1 incurred the wrath of Apophis, Hathor, Heru'ur, and Nirrti, an alternate reality provided the means to prevent a Goa'uld attack on Earth.

The SGC had established an observatory on Hanka.

HANKA

From an underground laboratory on Hanka, the Goa'uld Nirrti had conducted genetic experiments on the inhabitants to create a "hok'tar," or advanced human host. With SG-1's arrival, Nirrti concealed her experiments by unleashing a biological infection that killed the entire population except for Cassandra, a 12 year old girl in whom she had implanted a device intended to destroy Earth. Cassandra was rescued from the planet, and both the device and a dormant retrovirus within her were eventually neutralized. Cassandra remained on Earth as Dr. Fraiser's adopted daughter.

A biological infection had killed the entire population of 1432 people.

Juna Coordinates: 29-8-18-22-4-25

HARLAN

The biosphere of Altair had been destroyed by technology. Harlan, the last survivor of the planet, is a jovial soul in a synthetic body who had lived alone on Altair for more than 11,000 years. He created synthetic duplicates of SG-1 as companions to help him maintain the aging underground power facility that was his home. However, the synthetic duplicates continued to go on missions, and the duplicate team was destroyed during the joint battle with SG-1 to defeat Cronus and free Juna.

Underground facility on Altair (P3X-989)

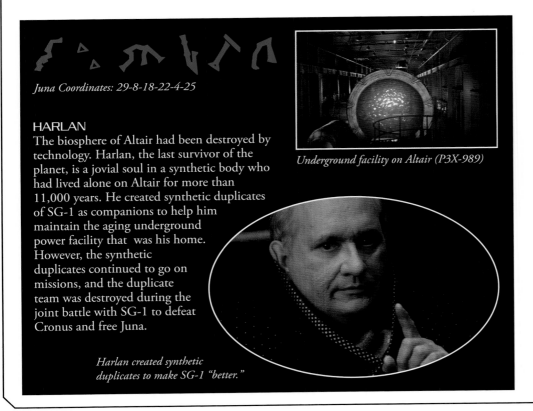

Harlan created synthetic duplicates to make SG-1 "better."

QUANTUM MIRROR

An abandoned laboratory on P3R-233 held a quantum mirror which allowed for inter-dimensional travel to alternate realities. Through it, Daniel found a reality where Earth faced annihilation from the Goa'uld, but a radio transmission from P3R-233 repeated, "Beware the Destroyers. They come from 3, 32, 16, 8, 10, 12," and held the key to preventing the same fate for Daniel's reality. The following year, an alternate Carter and Kawalsky arrived through the mirror, but following the mission to save their world, Hammond ordered that the mirror be destroyed.

LINEA

On the prison world of Hadante, SG-1 encountered Linea, whose brilliant scientific mind provided a means for their escape. However, they learned too late that Linea was the "Destroyer of Worlds," accused of causing a plague that devastated entire planets. Linea traveled to Vyus where her experiments to restore youth led to the Vorlix, a catastrophic accident in which the entire population became instantly young, with no memories of its past. Linea became Ke'ra, and she remained on Vyus after helping SG-1 to cure the global amnesia.

The Taldor of P3X-775 sentenced SG-1 to life imprisonment on Hadante.

Linea used cold fusion to power the stargate as she and SG-1 escaped.

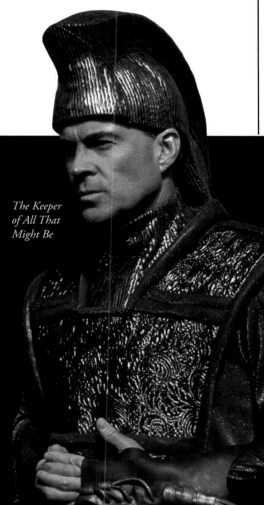

The Keeper of All That Might Be

P7J-989 had regenerated itself into a fertile garden world.

THE KEEPER

P7J-989 was destroyed by a chemical disaster 1022 years ago, and the inhabitants had placed themselves in suspended animation as the planet regenerated itself. Unique virtual reality chairs, monitored by the Keeper, had sustained the population, but when SG-1 became trapped in the devices, they found themselves reliving past moments of their lives for the entertainment of the Residents. Repeatedly, O'Neill experienced a failed mission in East Germany and Daniel witnessed the violent death of his parents until SG-1 found a means of release from the devices.

THE ORB

Millennia ago, P5C-353 was dying, and the native microscopic organisms created an orb where they slept for 100,000 years. Once exposed to the atmosphere of a living world on Earth, the orb activated, sending out spikes that impaled O'Neill in the gateroom, and the organisms went forth and multiplied. So it was written on the orb. Through O'Neill, the organisms were able to communicate, and they agreed to be sent to a primordial world where they could live and multiply.

SG-1 had believed the orb was a time capsule.

The microscopic organisms spoke through O'Neill.

Missions: Year 2

IN THE WAR AGAINST the Goa'uld, SG-1 had begun to encounter valuable allies and technologies. Highly advanced races, such as the Tollans, the Tok'ra, and the Asgard, had come to consider the Tauri as friends. In addition, SG-1 may have helped to shape their own destiny when their contact with Catherine Langford 30 years in the past helped to trigger her interest in renewing the research that would lead to the Stargate Program.

The Touchstone determines meteorological conditions for the entire planet.

MADRONA

The Madronans are a simple people who rely on the Touchstone, a device created by an advanced race about 900 years ago, to artificially control and maintain their weather. When rogue NID operatives stole the device, catastrophic weather conditions nearly destroyed the planet. The Madronans suspected that SG-1 was responsible for the theft, but they allowed the team to leave, trusting that they would recover the device and save Madrona from destruction. With the Touchstone restored, the planet and its people were saved.

A black hole formed near P3W-451.

BLACK HOLE

P3W-451 orbits the companion star of a newly formed black hole. As the intense gravity began to tear the planet apart, SG-10 could not escape, and the SGC was unable to break the connection to the singularity's gravitational field through the open wormhole. The resulting time dilation and extreme gravity threatened to draw all of Earth through the stargate until a deliberate wormhole arc allowed the stargate to disengage. P3W-451 was later used by Carter to create an artificial supernova.

SG-10 became trapped in a time dilation field.

MA'CHELLO

SG-1 encountered Ma'chello as a frail and elderly man, the only inhabitant of P3W-924. His laboratory contained inventions to fight the Goa'uld, including a personality transfer device with which he traded bodies with Daniel for a brief "holiday" on Earth. Following Ma'chello's death, SG-1 found his Goa'uld-killing inventions in the Linvris chamber on PY3-948. SG-1 became infected with the devices, which cause delusions and hallucinations in unblended humans, but the devices could be deactivated by an injection of a synthetic protein marker.

The personalities of Ma'chello and Daniel, and of O'Neill and Teal'c were accidentally transferred.

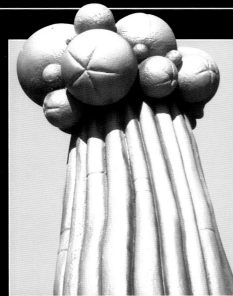

PJ2-445

PJ2-445 is inhabited by peaceful and innocent humanoid beings and by a complex network of plants. In a truly symbiotic relationship, the humanoid beings depend on an inaudible sound produced by the plants in order to live, and the plants respond to the unique trilling song of the humanoids. When injured by the UAV, the plants produced a sound of altered pitch which resulted in serious illness and death among the native beings until SG-1 could use frequency emitters to restore the balance of sound.

The plants can grow to several feet, and retract again into the ground.

The humanoids are silent except for a unique trilling sound.

THE REETOU

Reetalia was home to the Reetou, large insect-like creatures who are invisible in our phase. Most of the Reetou were destroyed by the Goa'uld, and in retaliation, Reetou rebels intend to defeat the Goa'uld through attrition by destroying all possible hosts. To warn Earth, the Reetou Authority created Charlie, a young genetically engineered human, to act as an intermediary. Although a squad of Reetou rebels infiltrated the SGC, the threat was eliminated with the help of the Tok'ra and TER weapons.

The Reetou exist 180° out of phase with Earth.

Charlie took his name from O'Neill's son.

1969

A massive solar flare sent SG-1 to August 4, 1969. There they were detained as suspected spies, but a young Lieutenant Hammond recognized his own writing on the note Carter had carried from the future, and he fulfilled his destiny by helping SG-1 to escape. Making their way cross country, SG-1 sought Catherine Langford and the stargate in Washington, DC, to use a second solar flare to send them back. Instead, a miscalculation flung them far into the future, where an adult Cassandra met the team and returned them home.

Michael and Jenny's psychedelic bus

A solar flare sent SG-1 thirty years into the past.

THE TOLLANS ARE A HIGHLY advanced race, capable of space travel, quilebrium physics, and duplicating stargate technology. Their civilization had not been at war for many generations, but overconfidence in their superior technology led to isolationism and an inability to think strategically. When Anubis developed shields impervious to the Tollan ion cannon, Tollana became vulnerable, and the Tollans were forced to reconsider their isolationist ways.

The Tollans cautiously welcomed diplomatic ties with Earth.

A network of ion cannons defended the modern cities.

NARIM

Narim was among the Tollan refugees who were rescued from the destruction of Tollan by SG-1. He became a spokesman in diplomatic relations with Earth, requesting the presence of SG-1 at the triad for Skaara. When Anubis and Tanith threatened Tollana, Narim risked his life and his planet to oppose them, which brought the wrath of the Goa'uld upon his world.

Narim alerted SG-1 to possible dangers following a suspicious death.

SCHRÖDINGER

Schrödinger, a cat given as a gift to Narim by Carter, was named for physicist Erwin Schrödinger.

ION CANNON

The Tollan ion cannon was the key weapon in the defense grid of Tollana. Linked in a network around the city, the enormous weapons could automatically target enemy ships. The Tollans had refused to share their technology with Earth, but when Anubis's advanced shields made his mothership impervious to the ion cannon, Tollana became vulnerable, and the Tollans offered Earth 38 ion cannons in exchange for trinium needed for weapons production. However their planet was destroyed before the trade was completed.

A single ion cannon could destroy a mothership in orbit.

Shared technology was the downfall of Tollan.

TOLLAN

Tollan, designated P3X-7763, had been the original homeworld of the Tollans. When the neighboring Saritans misused Tollan technology to make war, the cataclysmic devastation of Sarita led to orbital instability and intense volcanic activity on Tollan. The Tollans evacuated their world, barely escaping the destruction of their planet.

Coordinates: 6-33-27-37-11-18
Point of Origin: 2

Tanith

PHASE-SHIFT TECHNOLOGY

Tollan phase-shift technology allows objects to pass through solid matter. A Tollan device worn on the wrist generates a field enabling one to pass through walls. Trinium is required to house any device that generates the phase-shift technology. The Goa'uld forced the Tollan Curia to build weapons of mass destruction which employed phase-shift technology that would enable them to penetrate solid matter prior to detonation. The Goa'uld intended to use these weapons to penetrate Earth's iris, however the planet was destroyed by the Goa'uld when the Tollans refused to cooperate.

Phase-shift technology penetrates solid matter.

Coordinates: 4-29-8-22-18-25

Contact with Tollana was lost following Tanith's attack.

TOLLANA

The Tollan refugees established a new homeworld on Tollana. Despite modern cities, advanced technology, and a sophisticated defense network, Tollana fell victim to the Goa'uld when Tanith, in the service of Anubis, annihilated the cities from orbit.

TRAVELL

High Chancellor Travell was the head of the Curia, the highest governing body of Tollana. She welcomed formal diplomatic relations with Earth but staunchly refused to share Tollan technology. When Anubis threatened the destruction of Tollana, Travell and the Curia were forced by the Goa'uld to build weapons of mass destruction intended for use against Earth. However, the Tollans refused to cooperate, and Tanith launched an attack from orbit. The final transmission from Tollana reported widespread destruction and failing defenses, and the fate of their world is unknown.

The Tok'ra

TOK'RA LITERALLY means "Against Ra." The Tok'ra are a small alliance of Goa'uld resistance whose goal is the destruction of the System Lords. The great Queen Egeria had been a Goa'uld, but she broke from the empire over 2000 years ago and came to Earth to prevent the Goa'uld from taking human slaves. She was captured by Ra and secretly imprisoned in stasis for thousands of years on Pangar, but not before founding the Tok'ra movement through her offspring.

Egeria was discovered in stasis and revived on Pangar.

Garshaw of Belote and Cordesh of the Tok'ra High Council

PHYSIOLOGY

Goa'uld and Tok'ra share a physiology but differ in philosophy. The Tok'ra only blend with a host by choice, taking the gender of the host, and sharing a truly symbiotic relationship. A symbiote can double the lifespan of a host to nearly 200 years, and when a symbiote dies, it can choose to make the conscious effort to prevent the release of toxins that would kill its host.

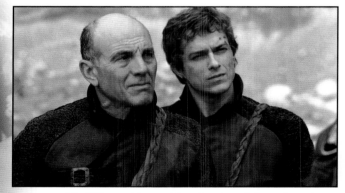

The Tok'ra symbiote and host share knowledge and emotions.

SOCIETY

Despite philosophical differences, the Tok'ra High Council has formalized the Earth-Tok'ra alliance with an official treaty. The Tok'ra are infiltrators who use disguise and subterfuge within the Goa'uld ranks rather than direct confrontation to achieve their goals. However, their secret bases are scattered, and a lack of willing hosts has led to diminishing numbers over the centuries.

Jolinar's memories led SG-1 to first encounter the Tok'ra on P34-353J.

Aldwin

Ren'al

Malek

JACOB CARTER

Jacob Carter, father of Samantha Carter and her brother Mark, had served in the US Air Force and was nearing retirement as a major general. His relationship with his children had been strained since the death of his wife in a tragic accident when Sam was a teenager. At an Air Force function in Washington, Jacob was reunited with his daughter as she prepared to receive the Air Medal, but he revealed that he had been recently diagnosed with lymphoma and his prognosis was not optimistic.

Jacob pilots a Goa'uld ha'tak.

SELMAK

Jacob was given only days to live when he agreed to become a host to Selmak, one of the oldest and wisest among the Tok'ra. By becoming Selmak's new host, Jacob's cancer was cured, and for six years he lived among the Tok'ra, taking on the role of ally and liaison to Earth.

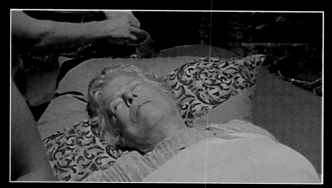

Selmak had shared the host body of Saroosh, but at the age of 203, Saroosh was dying.

DAKARA

At 2000 years old, Selmak was nearing the end of his life, and his health began to deteriorate. At Jacob's insistence, Selmak held on for several weeks so that his knowledge could help to defeat the Replicators at Dakara, however he slipped into a coma immediately afterward, and was unable to prevent the release of toxins that would kill his host. As Selmak slipped closer to death, Jacob's condition also weakened. Despite years of estrangement, Jacob and his daughter had grown closer than ever, and after bidding a gentle goodbye, Selmak and Jacob quietly passed away.

As a Tok'ra, Jacob acquired Selmak's knowledge and skills, and often cooperated with SG-1's missions.

The Tok'ra

ALTHOUGH THE TOK'RA have not readily shared intelligence, they have willingly shared their technology with Earth, and Tok'ra operatives such as Martouf, Anise, Aldwin, Ren'al, and Malek have regularly collaborated with the SGC. However, the Tok'ra are a race on the brink of extinction, and although they remain allies of Earth, recent losses have driven them to limit their contact with the Tauri.

MARTOUF & LANTASH
Martouf, the host to the symbiote Lantash, had been the mate of Jolinar for more than 100 years. When Martouf was programmed as a zatarc and killed, his symbiote was placed in stasis and later entered a wounded Lieutenant Elliot on Revanna. Surrounded by Jaffa, Elliot and Lantash sacrificed themselves to destroy Zipacna's army by releasing a symbiote poison.

Martouf and Carter

ANISE AND FREYA
Anise, whose name means "noble strength," is the symbiote within the host body of Freya. As an archaeologist with expertise in ancient cultures, Anise acted as a liaison to the SGC, and she offered limited cooperation, sharing such technology as the Atanik armbands and zatarc detector. Anise shared Daniel's intellectual interests, although Freya expressed her preference for O'Neill.

JOLINAR AND ROSHA
Jolinar of Malkshur was the symbiote within the host body of Rosha. An influential Tok'ra, she was captured by Sokar and imprisoned on Netu where she was brutally tortured before making her escape. As a fugitive from the System Lords, Jolinar fled to Nasya and took a male host, then left her dying host in battle and entered Carter. Found by the Ashrak on Earth, she was tortured by the harakash, and gave her life to save Carter, who still retains some of her memories, knowledge, and abilities.

Jolinar hid from the Ashrak by taking Carter as a host.

SG-1 assisted the Tok'ra with the evacuation of Vorash.

VORASH

Vorash, a barren, rocky, desert planet, had been used as a Tok'ra base. When the Tok'ra planned to relocate to a more secure base, they evacuated Vorash and intended to bring the stargate with them. However, SG-1 took the opportunity to use the stargate to create an artificial supernova from Vorash's sun in order to destroy Apophis's fleet, and the entire solar system was wiped out.

TOK'RA TUNNELS

When the Tok'ra arrive on a planet, they go deep underground and use technology to plant crystals which grow a network of tunnels, similar to a geode. Small square crystals create short straight openings, while diamond-shaped crystals tunnel toward the surface. When the Tok'ra abandon a planet, the process is reversed and the vanishing tunnels eliminate the network.

Individual crystals are specifically programmed to create different types of passageways.

REVANNA

Revanna became a Tok'ra base following the evacuation of Vorash, however it was annihilated by a fleet of motherships under the command of Zipacna, who served Anubis. During the invasion, the members of SG-17 lost their lives, and all of the Tok'ra on the base were killed, including Ren'al and Aldwin. Lieutenant Elliot, as the host to Lantash, remained behind to release the symbiote poison that would kill the invading army of Jaffa.

Since the crushing defeat of the Tok'ra at Revanna, only a fraction of their number remains.

The Asgard

THE ASGARD ARE A HIGHLY advanced and benevolent race, one of the four races of the Ancient Alliance. They resemble Roswell Greys, and have regularly monitored and studied human development on Earth. The Asgard inhabit many planets across their home galaxy and our own, and they protect more primitive cultures through technology and holographic images which take on the role of Norse gods to guide the planet's development.

Knowledge from the Ancient repository on P3R-272 led O'Neill to encounter the Asgard on Othala.

PHYSIOLOGY
As a species, the Asgard are a dying race. They reproduce exclusively through cloning, and as each Asgard's body fails, his consciousness is transferred into a younger cloned version of himself. However, thousands of years of cloning have caused genetic deterioration which could lead to the fall of Asgard civilization.

SOCIETY
The Asgard High Council had designated worlds such as Cimmeria and K'tau as protected from the Goa'uld under the Protected Planets Treaty. However, the Asgard faced a far more dangerous enemy in the Replicators, a plague that stretched across their home galaxy. Asgard overconfidence in their own technology has been their undoing, and several times they have turned to Earth for help in defeating their enemy.

The Daniel Jackson, *an Asgard mothership.*

FREYR
Freyr, a member of the Asgard High Council, protects the planet K'tau in the persona of Lord of the Aesir, Norse god of sun and rain, and ruler of the elves. Through the Hall of Wisdom, SG-1 sought help from Freyr and the Council to restore the K'tau sun and to prevent the asteroid collision with Earth, but both requests were denied due to restrictions of the Protected Planets Treaty. SG-1 assisted the Asgard when Freyr requested their help to rescue Heimdall and Thor from Anubis in the Adara System.

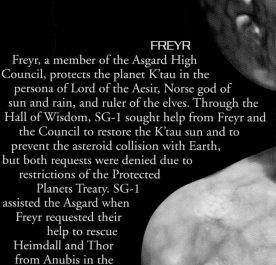

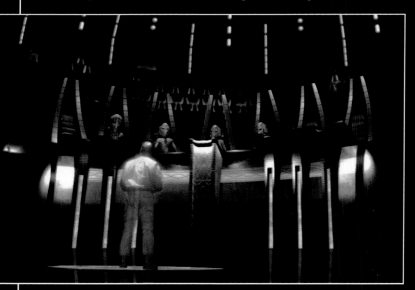

SG-1 communicated with the Asgard High Council via live holographic images.

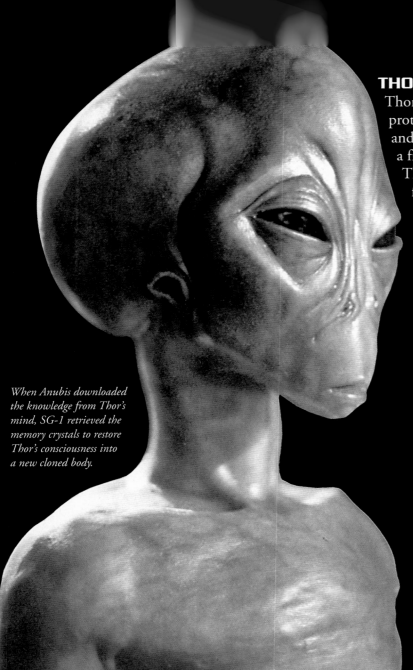

THOR

Thor had brought humans from Earth to Cimmeria and protected them from the Goa'uld by taking on the persona and holographic representation of the imposing Norse god, a friend to humans and a powerful warrior whose weapon, Thor's Hammer, produced lightning and thunder. SG-1 first encountered the Asgard when they proved themselves worthy in the Hall of Thor's Might on Cimmeria, and Thor revealed himself in his true Asgard form.

When Anubis downloaded the knowledge from Thor's mind, SG-1 retrieved the memory crystals to restore Thor's consciousness into a new cloned body.

Thor is both a military leader and gifted scientist.

SUPREME COMMANDER

Thor is the Supreme Commander of the Asgard Fleet and a member of the Asgard High Council. From his legendary motherships, the *Biliskner*, the *O'Neill*, and the *Daniel Jackson*, he has battled the Asgard's greatest enemies, the Goa'uld and the Replicators. As a true ally of Earth, he negotiated with the System Lords for Earth's inclusion in the Protected Planets Treaty, and several times he has turned to SG-1 for help in defeating the Replicators. In gratitude, Thor has shared Asgard technology including shields, weapons, beam technology, and a hyperdrive for use on the *Prometheus*.

HEIMDALL

Heimdall, an Asgard scientist, has been conducting vital research into genetic manipulation designed to stave off the degradation of cloning technology and to preserve the Asgard race. His research is based on the recent discovery near the Adara System of an Asgard ship lost 30,000 years ago, carrying an ancient crew preserved in stasis. When his underground laboratory came under attack from Osiris and Anubis, SG-1 rescued Heimdall and his research.

Heimdall's secret underground research facility in the Adara System

The Asgard

THE ASGARD HAVE COLONIZED and protected many worlds, and they have shown a willingness to share certain technologies with their allies. Advanced Asgard technology has included legendary motherships, transportation beams, sophisticated cloaking and invisibility devices, holographic projection, genetic manipulation and cloning technology, stasis pods, anti-gravity devices, and the ability to control the stargate without a DHD.

Loki was apprehended by SG-1.

LOKI

Loki, the Norse god of mischief, is an Asgard geneticist who had abducted humans from Earth, hoping to use human physiology as a template to improve Asgard cloning technology. Loki created clones to temporarily replace each abductee, however clones suffered from genetic deterioration due to Loki's inept methods, and rarely lived beyond a week. Loki's abductions had ceased 19 years ago when he was banished for his unsanctioned experiments.

Young O'Neill believed himself to be the real O'Neill who had been inexplicably regressed in age.

YOUNG JACK O'NEILL

Hoping that O'Neill's advanced DNA held the key to Asgard cloning, Loki secretly returned to Earth. He abducted O'Neill and created a replacement clone, however the clone failed to mature properly. Young Jack O'Neill aged to only 15 years, and, like Loki's previous clones, would live only a few days. When Loki was apprehended, Thor repaired the young clone's DNA, enabling him to mature at a normal human rate.

HALA

Hala, in the Asgard home galaxy, was the original Asgard homeworld until it was evacuated and used to lure the Replicators. Here the Replicators evolved into human form and were trapped within a time dilation field. Two years later, Thor collapsed Hala's sun, creating a black hole which destroyed the planet, however the Replicators were able to escape from the event horizon.

Hala became an unwelcoming environment, paved with Replicator blocks.

Othala has also been used as the name of the galaxy in which Hala and Orilla are located.

The beams are capable of transporting individual people or objects as large as a stargate.

ASGARD TRANSPORT BEAM

The Asgard molecular transportation device uses a beam to transport objects instantaneously over significant distances. Extremely versatile, the beam uses sensors to pinpoint specific targets and usually appears as a sudden vertical flash or as a moving ray of light within which objects materialize or dematerialize. Asgard beams have been installed on the *Prometheus*, and certain enemies, including the Trust, the Goa'uld, and the Replicators have acquired the technology.

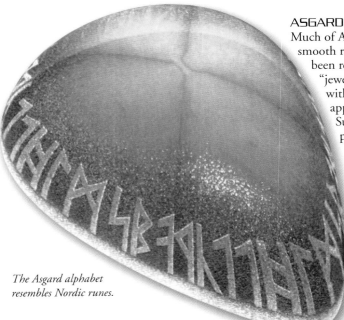

The Asgard alphabet resembles Nordic runes.

ASGARD STONES

Much of Asgard technology is based on smooth rounded devices which have been referred to as "stones" or "jewels." Often they are inscribed with Asgard runic symbols and appear to glow when functioning. Such stones, moved in specific positions on a control panel, have been used to control many functions of an Asgard mothership, including communications, holographic projection, navigation, transport beams, and information retrieval.

Asgard stones can be used as voice activated communication devices.

The new colony of Orilla became the last chance of rebuilding the Asgard civilization.

OTHALA

Othala, a legendary Norse ruin, is also an Asgard homeworld in the galaxy of Ida. Because of Othala's distance, the stargate requires additional power and a gate address of 8 glyphs to make a connection. Using the knowledge of the Ancients, O'Neill reached Othala, where he encountered the Asgard for the first time.

Coordinates: 11-27-23-16-33-3-9

ORILLA

Following the evacuation of Hala, the Asgard built a new colony on Orilla. The planet is rich in neutronium, an element essential to both Asgard technology and to the creation of human-form Replicators. Fifth and the Replicators sought the vital element, but the new disruptor weapon prevented their invasion.

 # STORY ARCS

SG-1 discovers the beta stargate in Antarctica, and Heliopolis, the Library of the Four Races.

O'Neill temporarily acquires the knowledge of the Ancients from the Ancient repository.

On Kheb, SG-1 encounters Oma Desala, an ascended Ancient who raises the Harsesis child.

Apophis steps through the Earth stargate, and the war with the Goa'uld begins.

Apophis's attack on Earth fails. SG-1 confronts Heru'ur, Sokar, and Hathor. Apophis fathers the Harsesis child.

Heru'ur and Cronus are killed, Osiris is awakened from stasis, and Apophis dominates the System Lords.

Cronus, Nirrti, and Yu negotiate the Protected Planets Treaty. Hathor, Seth, and Sokar are killed.

SG-1 wins a small victory against the Replicators on Earth and on the Asgard homeworld.

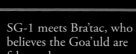

SG-1 meets the Asgard when Thor reveals himself in his true form and O'Neill is drawn to Othala.

Thor facilitates the negotiation with the Goa'uld to include Earth in the Protected Planets Treaty.

Thor seeks SG-1's help to defeat the Replicators in the Asgard home galaxy.

SG-1 meets Bra'tac, who believes the Goa'uld are false gods.

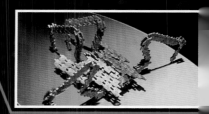

SG-1 meets the Tok'ra and an alliance is formed when Jacob Carter becomes a host to Selmak.

Senator Kinsey attempts to cut off funding and shut down the Stargate Program.

Colonel Maybourne oversees rogue NID missions using the beta stargate on Earth.

Rogue NID operatives are apprehended and convicted of treason, but rogue NID missions continue.

Colonel Maybourne is released from prison and cooperates with O'Neill in uncovering evidence of NID activities.

SG-1 encounters Orlin, an ascended Ancient, and Oma Desala helps to guide Daniel Jackson to ascension.

Ayiana, a living Ancient, is discovered in Antarctica, and an Ancient tablet leads to a Lost City.

Daniel descends to human form. The knowledge of the Ancients leads SG-1 to a ZPM and an Ancient weapon that defeats Anubis.

The Ancient weapon on Dakara defeats the Replicators, and Oma Desala confronts Anubis for eternity.

Ba'al captures O'Neill, and Nirrti is killed. Anubis attacks Earth, destroys Abydos, and defeats the forces of the System Lords.

Anubis raises an army of Kull Warriors and dominates the System Lords, but is defeated in the battle over Antarctica.

Ba'al dominates the System Lords, who face defeat by the Replicators. Anubis is caught in eternal struggle with Oma Desala.

Apophis is killed by the Replicators, and Anubis rises to power at the Summit of the System Lords at Hassara.

Fifth escapes and creates Replicator Carter, who destroys him. The weapon on Dakara rids the galaxy of the Replicators.

SG-1 encounters Reese, who once created the Replicators but who no longer has the ability to control them.

The Replicators evolve into human form and are trapped in a time dilation field on Hala.

Thor defeats the Replicators at Orilla, and assists SG-1 to modify the disruptor technology as Replicators invade the galaxy.

SG-1 encounters Freyr and comes to the aid of Heimdall and Thor when they become the targets of Anubis.

SG-1 rescues Thor's consciousness from Anubis, and helps Thor to trap the Replicators in a time dilation field on Hala.

The Rebel Jaffa defeat the Goa'uld at Dakara and claim the holy site as the new Jaffa nation.

Bra'tac and Teal'c follow K'tano as he raises an army and the Jaffa Rebellion begins.

The Rebel movement grows and forms an uneasy alliance with the Tok'ra. Rebel leaders are slaughtered at the Ambush of Kresh'taa.

The Hak'tyl join the Rebel movement, and the alliance with the Tok'ra begins to crumble.

Jacob and Selmak assist in defeating the Replicators at Dakara, but as Selmak dies, Jacob also passes away.

SG-1 encounters Egeria, the founder of the Tok'ra movement. O'Neill becomes a temporary host to Kanan.

Jacob maintains contact with Earth even as the alliance with the Tauri and the Rebel Jaffa begins to crumble.

The Trust acquires an alkesh and symbiote poison, but is compromised by the Goa'uld. Kinsey becomes a Goa'uld host.

Colonel Simmons arrives at the SGC with a secret NID agenda, and he takes custody of Adrian Conrad.

Rogue NID operatives hijack the *Prometheus*, Senator Kinsey is shot, and members of the Committee are apprehended.

Kinsey becomes vice president and attempts to use the power of the White House to seize control of the SGC.

SG-1 EXPERIENCED POIGNANT reunions and painful loss as Daniel was reunited with his grandfather and with Skaara but faced the death of Sha're. Yet Sha're's words guided the team to Kheb, and the first encounter with the Ancients. On Earth, the insidious shadow organization within the NID continued to grow, and SG-1 confronted an even more ominous foe—the Replicators.

Aliens from P3X-118

Coordinates: 9-26-34-37-17-21

FOOTHOLD

Aliens from P3X-118 established a foothold situation, or alien incursion, on Earth. By wearing small electronic mimic devices, the aliens could duplicate the appearance and access the thoughts of SGC personnel, who were kept alive in suspended animation. The incursion was averted and 12 mimic devices were recovered for study.

SGC personnel were kept in suspended animation.

The Orbanians may be descendants of the pre-Aztec civilization of Teotihuacan.

ORBAN

From Merrin, an 11 year old girl from Orban, Carter acquired the technology for Earth's first naquadah reactor. On Orban, special urrone children such as Merrin use nanites to acquire knowledge, learning through nano-technology, then passing on their knowledge at age 12 through the averium, a ceremony in which an urrone's nanites are removed. Education was unknown on Orban until Merrin's averium passed on her experiences of Earth's schools to her people.

Aris Boch's race physically rejects Goa'uld symbiotes and cannot be used as hosts.

ARIS BOCH

Aris Boch is one of the galaxy's greatest bounty hunters. His world had been conquered by the Goa'uld, who caused the population to become addicted to roshna, a blue liquid substance which kept them subservient. As a bounty hunter for Sokar, Boch trades for the roshna he needs to live. On PJ6-877, Boch captured SG-1 while searching for Korra, a Tok'ra operative, but, after a change of heart, he granted Korra and SG-1 their freedom.

Laira had hoped that O'Neill would give her a child.

EDORA

Edora's orbit passes through an asteroid belt, causing a meteor shower, or "fire rain," each year, and an impact event approximately once every 150 years. During SG-1's visit, much of the population evacuated through the stargate as meteorites struck the planet, but the stargate was buried, leaving O'Neill and the survivors stranded for three months until a way to reopen the gate was discovered.

Coordinates: 28-38-35-9-15-3

Edora (P5C-768), a simple world with valuable naquadah resources.

URGO

Togar, of P4X-884, implanted a microscopic device into the brains of SG-1, designed to experience alien cultures vicariously. Urgo, the virtual personality associated with the device, appeared to SG-1 as a result of an error. Both endearing and annoying, Urgo was also self aware, and SG-1 convinced Togar to transfer the implant into his own brain so that Urgo could continue to live, experience the universe, and eat pie.

Invisible to other SGC personnel, Urgo was an ebullient personality with ceaseless enthusiasm and a childlike curiosity.

Nicholas Ballard remained on P7X-377 to exchange knowledge with the giant aliens.

CRYSTAL SKULL

The crystal skull of P7X-377, identical to the skull discovered by Nicholas Ballard in Belize, is a teleportation device. Looking into the eyes of the skull creates an energy field which transports one to an alternate phase of invisibility, the realm of the native giant aliens of the world.

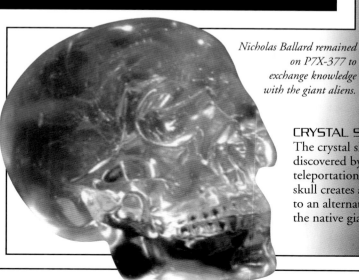

Quetzalcoatl, an ancient Mayan god, rose out of the mist.

The Replicators

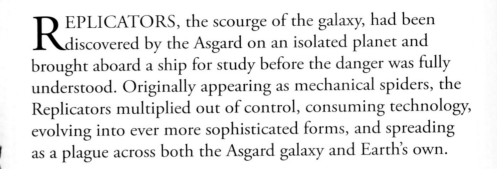

EPLICATORS, the scourge of the galaxy, had been discovered by the Asgard on an isolated planet and brought aboard a ship for study before the danger was fully understood. Originally appearing as mechanical spiders, the Replicators multiplied out of control, consuming technology, evolving into ever more sophisticated forms, and spreading as a plague across both the Asgard galaxy and Earth's own.

Individual kiron-based blocks

PHYSIOLOGY

Replicators are a kiron-based technology. Individual blocks exert a reactive modulating energy field on other blocks which allows them to assemble themselves in many forms, ultimately for the single purpose of self replication. They ingest metals and alloys, continually creating more of themselves and seeking more advanced technologies which they consume and modify to meet their needs. Replicators have an extremely high capacity for learning, and with each evolution they became more dangerous and indestructible.

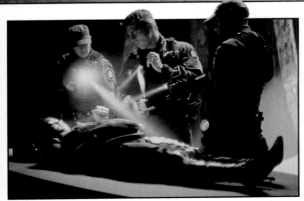

Left alone, Reese had put herself to sleep.

REESE

Reese was a sophisticated but childlike android who used the nano-technology of her design to create the first Replicators as toys that she could control with her mind. However, as she taught her toys to replicate and protect her, she began to lose control. The Replicators destroyed everyone on her world and left through the stargate. SG-1 brought Reese to Earth, but as she created new toys, O'Neill was forced to destroy her to prevent the Replicators' spread on Earth.

Reese created the Replicators as toys.

FIRST

The Asgard used Reese's technology to lure the Replicators to the planet Hala, however the Replicators recognized Reese's superior design and used it to evolve into human form.

Six human-form Replicators were created, and they took their names from the order in which they were made. Their leader, First, planned to go forward with his brethren as an army, but an Asgard device trapped the Replicators within a time dilation field on Hala.

The first human-form Replicator

Fifth's humanity allowed him to feel love, betrayal, and revenge.

FIFTH

Fifth was the fifth of the human-form Replicators, and the only one to have the flaw of compassion. He was betrayed by his own humanity when he agreed to help SG-1, but he later escaped from Hala, and in his conflicted feelings of love and revenge, he captured Carter and created a new human-form Replicator in her image. Once again Fifth was betrayed when Replicator Carter, who saw him as weak and unworthy, destroyed her creator and ruled in his place.

Fifth held Carter prisoner aboard his ship.

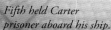

Fifth's Replicator Ship

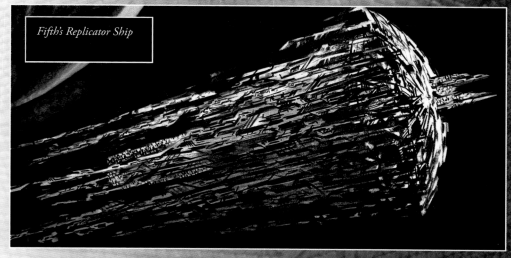

REPLICATOR CARTER

Fifth had created a human-form Replicator in the image of Samantha Carter, but although she shared Carter's knowledge and memories, she was ruthless and calculating, and was intent on galactic domination. She deceived SG-1 to obtain the cipher that made her immune to disruptor technology, and betrayed Fifth by using the disruptor to destroy him. Then she led her brethren across the Milky Way galaxy, systematically absorbing the forces of the System Lords.

DAKARA

As Replicator Carter controlled the army of Replicators with her mind, she sent them to invade Earth and to conquer the forces of Ba'al and the Rebel Jaffa at Dakara, the location of the one weapon capable of destroying her. When the Ancient device on Dakara was activated, the energy wave that translated throughout the galaxy instantly disintegrated every Replicator into individual harmless blocks. The enemy that had plagued the galaxies for generations was at last eliminated.

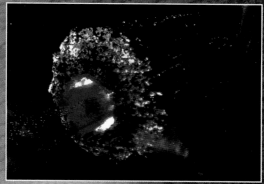

The Replicator ship was instantly dis...

A human-form Replicator in Carter's image

The Unas

UNAS IS A SPECIES NATIVE TO P3X-888, where both primordial Goa'uld and aboriginal Unas evolved. Those who were first taken as Goa'uld hosts learned to use the stargate and left the planet. The others remained and took refuge in the caves as protection against blending. Unas are incredibly strong and very territorial. Because they were the original hosts of the Goa'uld, they are known as "The First Ones," creatures who have become almost mythical.

Unas have been trained as slaves.

CHAKA

Chaka, one of the aboriginal Unas of P3X-888, captured Daniel as part of a rite of passage, but through rudimentary communication, the two developed a mutual respect, and he allowed Daniel to go free. When Chaka was kidnapped and taken off-world to a planet where Unas were bred as slaves, SG-1 followed and rescued him. Instead of returning home, however, Chaka insisted on remaining. He led an uprising and eventually brokered a truce which over time established a fragile but successful peace between the humans of the planet and the Unas who were formerly their slaves.

IRON SHIRT

The alpha male of the indigenous Unas of P3X-403 uses the name "Kor Asek," which translates from the Unas as "Iron Shirt." When an SGC mining operation desecrated the sacred burial grounds of the Unas ancestors, Iron Shirt led the resistance against the invaders. Daniel enlisted the help of Chaka to negotiate a truce, and although Iron Shirt was hesitant to trust the outsiders, he accepted the opportunity to honor the dead by helping to defeat the Goa'uld who had killed his ancestors. The Unas agreed to work the mine themselves, and to turn over the naquadah to the SGC.

Kor Asek, leader of 44 Unas tribes

Green Blood

Four Clawed Fingers

Aboriginal Unas

Ritualistic killing served as a warning to invaders.

P3X-403

The SGC was unaware of the indigenous Unas when it established a naquadah mining operation on P3X-403. When a resonance scan revealed 53,000 metric tons of the ore, the Unas attacked to protect their sacred grounds. They captured Lieutenant Ritter, staking him out in a ritualistic killing. The SGC intended to forcibly relocate the Unas, however Daniel, Chaka, and Iron Shirt succeeded in negotiating a peaceful solution.

The SGC established a mining operation.

P3X-888

P3X-888 is a primordial world, the aboriginal home to both the Goa'uld and the Unas. Both primitive species can still be found on the planet, the Goa'uld symbiotes infesting the rivers, and unblended Unas dwelling in caves. P3X-888 was the home planet of Chaka, who captured and befriended Daniel. Daniel later used remote surveillance cameras and continued to monitor the planet in order to study Unas culture and language.

P3X-888 has two moons.

Chaka captured Daniel as a rite of passage, but freed him in an act of friendship.

FACT FILE

UNAS DICTIONARY

The language of the Unas of P3X-888 uses a very simple structure and words that can have various meanings depending on the context in which they are used.

A (a)	the, and, or, of, a, because
Aka (a ka')	thank you
Asek (a sek')	shirt, top, overgarment
Benna (ben na')	kneel, retreat, surrender, submissive
Cha'aka (cha a ka')	god be with you, formal thank you, sorry
Cho'ee'che (choe ee' chay)	don't know, maybe, learn, negotiate
Ka (ka)	no, not, opposite, different, other
Ka cha (ka chaa')	go, travel, journey, move
Kada (ka' da)	naquadah
Ka nay (ka nay')	friend, fellow tribe or clan member
Ka nayA (ka nay a')	tribe
Keka (ke' aka)	kill, death, dead, danger, watch out
Kekata (ke ka' ta)	staff weapon
Kel (kel)	what, who, where, when, why
Ko (koe)	give, take, transfer
Kor (kore)	iron, metal, strong, hard
Kreeka (kree' ka)	attack, take action, attention
Lota (Loe ta')	wait
Ma kan (ama kaan')	yes, good, okay, happy, agreement
Nan (naan)	eat, food
Nok (nawk)	now, new, young, present
No na (no' naa)	home, territory, planet
Onac (oe' nawk)	goa'uld, oppressor, enemy
Seseka (se se' kaa')	22 from a base 8 number system
Soseka (soe se kaa')	44 from a base 8 number system
Shesh (shesh)	alarm, what is it?
Ska nat (skaa naat')	preserve life, selfless, noble
Ta (taa)	you, yours, they
Tak (taak)	trick, dishonesty
Tar (taar)	human, host
Te (tay)	I, I have, me, we
Tok (toke)	against, struggle, fight, resist
Tonok (ton' awk)	fear, intimidation
Wok tah (wawk' taa')	marked for death
Zo (zoe)	term of respect, leader, honor, alpha

The Aschen

Mollem

Borren

O'Neill distrusted the Aschen.

THE ASCHEN ARE A HIGHLY advanced race from P4C-970, but their technological advancements conceal a sinister agenda. A very patient people, the Aschen seek new worlds to colonize, and share their technology while offering a life-extending drug that causes sterility in humans. Within a few generations the planet's native population is wiped out and the world falls under Aschen control.

2010

In July of 2010, SG-1 was preparing to celebrate the tenth anniversary of their first mission to P4C-970 which had led to their alliance with the Aschen and Earth's membership in the Aschen Confederation.

SG-1 celebrates the tenth anniversary of the Aschen Alliance.

ASCHEN CONFEDERATION

Under the Aschen alliance, the Goa'uld had been defeated and Earth was at peace. Aschen advancements in medicine had developed an anti-aging vaccine which caused a 91% drop in the birthrate, but the population was unaware that humanity was on the brink of extinction.

When the retired members of SG-1 realized the Aschen's insidious plot to conquer Earth, they devised a plan to use time travel to change their own fate. SG-1 sent a message through the stargate to themselves ten years in the past, to prevent the Aschen alliance. The note read, "Under no circumstances go to P4C-970. Colonel Jack O'Neill," and although SG-1 was killed in the attempt to breach security, the message was successfully sent, history was changed, and humanity was saved.

SG-1 is honored for bringing about the Aschen Alliance.

The note from the future.

SG-1 receives the mysterious note.

O'Neill breaches Aschen security.

AMBASSADOR JOSEPH FAXON

Joseph Faxon, who had been chosen to negotiate a trade agreement with the Aschen, developed a fondness for Carter. In one version of history, he and Carter were married, and he maintained an important position as Earth's off-world ambassador under the Aschen Confederation. When history was altered by the warning note from the future, Faxon's negotiations uncovered the Aschen duplicity, and he gave Carter a chance to escape, remaining behind on P3A-194 as a prisoner of the Aschen.

In 2010, Joseph Faxon and Carter were married.

MOLLEM

In an alternate future, Mollem, a scientist and leading member of the Aschen, held a position of influence on Earth under the Aschen Confederation. By changing history and preventing contact with P4C-970, SG-1 encountered Mollem instead on P3A-194 where he conducted negotiations for a trade agreement with Earth. When the Aschen scheme to sterilize the population was exposed and negotiations were abruptly ended, Mollem attempted to send a bio-weapon through Earth's stargate, but his attempt failed when the weapon did not penetrate the iris.

The Aschen use floating harvesters on P3A-194.

VOLIANS

Two hundred years ago, the Volians of P3A-194 were a thriving urban civilization. They welcomed the Aschen to their world and willingly joined the Confederation. But when the Aschen agenda was exposed, there were riots, the urban society abruptly ended, and all evidence of the past was buried. In 200 years P3A-194 went from an urban civilization of millions to a simple agrarian civilization of thousands.

The Aschen attempted to send a bio-weapon to Earth.

The Volians are simple farmers with no memory of their planet's past.

A S THE SYSTEM LORDS continued to vie for power and Apophis rose to a position of dominance, SG-1 confronted obstacles in the search for allies and technology. Fragile alliances with the Tok'ra and the Russians proved tenuous, research into devices such as the zatarc detector, Atanik armbands, and X-301 spacecraft lacked promise, and worlds such as Euronda and P3R-118 that offered hope, instead held unexpected perils.

EURONDA

The Eurondans offered advanced technology in exchange for assistance in a bitter civil war, but their true agenda was exposed. They called their enemy "Breeders," because they reproduce with no regard for genetic purity, and the Eurondans had poisoned the planet's surface as a military tactic to exterminate them. The Eurondans hoped to reclaim their unlivable world with SG-1's help, but they were denied and left to perish as their defenses crumbled.

Coordinates: 30-27-9-7-18-16

The Eurondans sought SG-1's help.

Apophis's new battleship on PX9-757

Malikai had hoped to be with his wife once more.

TIME LOOP

P4X-639 was once a colony of the Ancients. To avoid a cataclysm, the inhabitants built a time machine to change their own history, but the device never worked and in the end they perished. Malikai, an archaeologist, discovered the device on the long-deserted planet, and inadvertently caught Earth and 12 other worlds in a continuous subspace time loop for over three months before SG-1 convinced him to abandon his quest.

ATANIKS

The Ataniks, an ancient race, were the creators of unique armbands, long thought to be a myth, which give the wearer incredible speed and strength. SG-1 tested the devices and relied on their enhanced abilities during a mission to destroy Apophis's new battleship on PX9-757. However, the armbands release a virus to access the human physiology, and the body's immune system eventually rejects them. This flaw, which had led to the extinction of the Ataniks, also jeopardized SG-1's mission, and the armbands were abandoned.

Atanik armbands work for a limited time.

O'Neill and Teal'c realized that time was repeating.

ENKARANS

As SG-1 helped the Enkarans to establish a new homeworld on P5S-381, an automated ship of the Gadmeer race began terraforming the planet to support a sulfur-based ecosystem. Unable to halt the process, both races faced extinction on a single world. Negotiations with Lotan, a bio-mechanical representation of the Gadmeer ship, led to the discovery of the original Enkaran homeworld to which the Enkarans could be relocated.

A vast curtain of energy terraformed the planet.

Lotan was created by the Gadmeer ship.

P3R-118

On P3R-118, Administrator Calder and his people lived in comfort in a domed city while those chosen as workers were given new identities through memory stamp technology and labored in the underground power facility. Calder resented SG-1's judgment of his world, and the team was detained and forced to join the workers, taking new identities as Jona, Therra, Carlin, and Tor. Once their memories returned, SG-1 released the workers, forcing the city dwellers to support themselves.

P3R-118 is a planet in the midst of an ice age.

MARTIN LLOYD

When Martin's homeworld had been attacked by the Goa'uld, he and four comrades had sought allies, but instead they abandoned their ship and began anew, living incognito in Montana. Martin appeared to SG-1 as a science fiction fanatic and conspiracy theorist until the discovery of his devastated homeworld verified his stories. He settled in Hollywood and sold a screenplay for "Wormhole X-treme!" a cable TV series based on the SGC.

Martin's Homeworld: 24-12-32-7-11-34

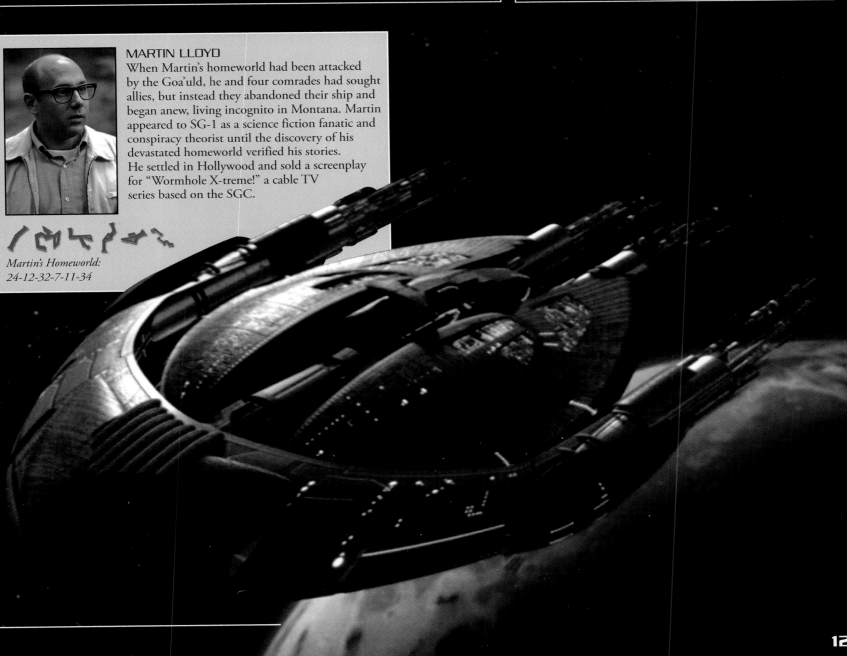

AT THE SUMMIT of the System Lords, an ominous new threat arose as Anubis began his conquest of the galaxy. Tollana and the Tok'ra fell to his superior forces, and the Protected Planets Treaty began to crumble, leaving worlds such as K'tau and Earth vulnerable. Naquadria offered promise as a potential new weapon, but the mission to Kelowna instead brought the devastating loss of Daniel Jackson.

THE LIGHT

A long abandoned Goa'uld pleasure palace on P4X-347 contains a pedestal which projects a strangely addictive light-matrix hologram onto the ceiling. The planet's sole inhabitant was Loran, a young man whose parents had come as explorers and had died from the addictive effects of the light. Loran helped SG-1 disable the device to gradually withdraw from their own addiction, and he returned to Earth with them, leaving the planet abandoned once more.

The light triggered instantaneous addiction and critical withdrawal and depression.

M4C-862

A research station was established on M4C-862, a moon 42,000 light years from Earth. The small, glowing, energy-based life-forms native to the moon exhibited intelligent behavior and could pass through solid matter, but an electromagnetic field could contain or repel them. Harmless at first, they later gathered in swarms and attacked, forcing the team to evacuate. The change in their behavior from benign to violent may have been retaliatory due to the capture of one of their own.

Cadet Jennifer Hailey and Carter examine a captured energy being.

Energy beings can pass through solid matter.

Coordinates:
25-8-18-29-4-22

ENTITY

MALP transmissions were a contagion to the electrically-based life-forms of P9C-372, and an "entity" returned through the open wormhole, intent on preserving its own world by destroying Earth. It established an electronic "nest" within the base computer mainframe, and took Carter as a host through whom it could communicate. In fear of O'Neill's threat of retaliation, however, it chose to spare its world by sacrificing itself. The entity transferred Carter's consciousness into its nest before releasing her body, allowing Carter's life to be restored.

REOL

The Reol are a peaceful race whose natural defense mechanism is a chemical produced in their bodies which causes one to perceive their alien appearance as quite human and familiar. When Kaiael crashed on P7S-441, he used the defense mechanism and the "Made in Tyler, Texas" label from an MRE to induce SG-1's memory of him as Lieutenant Tyler, from Texas, a member of SG-1. The Tok'ra have since synthesized a modified version of the Reol chemical that can be used to disguise one's identity during undercover missions.

The Reol conceal their true appearance with a chemical that triggers memory centers of the brain.

Coordinates: 18-2-30-12-26-33

K'TAU

On K'tau, Elrad welcomed SG-1 as elves, but Malchus distrusted them as harbingers of doom. When the K'tau sun inexplicably shifted to the infrared light spectrum and threatened life on the planet, Carter theorized that introducing the superheavy element HU2340 into the sun's core might reverse the crisis, but the deeply religious people declined SG-1's help, relying instead on prayer to their god Freyr. The sun was mysteriously restored, however whether the correction was due to science or faith is uncertain.

Malchus and Elrad are religious leaders of K'tau, an Asgard protected world with Nordic roots.

The inscription on the Sentinel reads, "Life Energy—Two As One."

LATONA

The Sentinel, an advanced planetary defensive weapon, had protected the peaceful inhabitants of Latona for over 300 years. The device is activated when a human caretaker joins his life energy with that of the machine, but when rogue NID operatives attempted to steal the technology and killed the caretaker, Latona was left defenseless. SG-1 attempted to restore the device, and the invading forces of Svarog were destroyed when Colonel Grieves activated the Sentinel by joining with it in the caretaker's place.

Kelowna

Kelowna is an industrialized nation.

KELOWNA IS ONE OF three major nations on P2S-4C3. About 15 years ago the Kelownans discovered an ancient temple of the Goa'uld Thanos, who had occupied the planet thousands of years ago. Within the temple they found a stargate, as well as artifacts, writings, and naquadria, a powerful radioactive mineral which they began developing as a weapon, despite evidence that similar experiments had destroyed their planet 10,000 years ago. Kelowna is the homeworld of Jonas Quinn, who defected to Earth following the devastating lab accident that took the life of Daniel Jackson.

NAQUADRIA PROJECT

Naquadria, a heavier, highly unstable, radioactive isotope of naquadah, does not occur in nature but was converted from raw naquadah by Thanos. The Kelownan Naquadria Project used the mineral for weapons technology research, and when Dr. Kieran's team tested a naquadria bomb, its destructive power exceeded all expectations. Although the device was considered a weapon of last resort, when faced with destruction in a global war, the Kelownans used the weapon against their enemies with devastating results.

Kelowna's Naquadria Weapon

Jonas shared naquadria research with SG-1.

Commander Hale, leader of Kelowna

ANUBIS

Anubis captured Jonas Quinn, and through a mind probe gained all of Jonas's knowledge of his homeworld. Determined to acquire naquadria technology, Anubis turned his attention to Kelowna. Commander Hale had hoped to spare Kelowna by meeting Anubis's demands, but his negotiation only betrayed his world, and Anubis launched an invasion. The planet was spared when Anubis's fleet was defeated in battle by Ba'al and the United Alliance of the System Lords.

A lab accident exposed Daniel to lethal radiation.

Anubis's mothership hovers over Kelowna.

The United Alliance of the System Lords defeated Anubis.

LANGARA

Kelowna, Tirania, and the Andari Federation, the three major powers of the P2S-4C3, have historically quarreled over grievances that go back generations. Following the threats to their world from the detonation of the naquadria weapon and the battle with Anubis, the nations agreed to an uneasy peace, and formed a Joint Ruling Council. They chose "Langara" as the new name of their world, a name meant to be a symbol of their new unity, but decades of animosity were not easily overcome and relations between bickering delegates remained strained.

Lucia Tarthus of the Andari

Vin Eremal of Tirania

Minister Dreylock of Kelowna

P2S-4C3 became known as Langara.

DR. KIERAN

Dr. Kieran, a professor and researcher at the Academy of Science, headed the Naquadria Project until he began to exhibit increasingly erratic behavior, claiming that a secret underground resistance on Kelowna was poised to seize power. Dr. Kieran's exposure to naquadria radiation had caused a unique form of brain damage, and he was diagnosed with advanced schizophrenia. The Kelownan resistance was merely a manifestation of his illness. Dr. Kieran was brought to Earth for treatment, but his condition was irreversible.

Deep Underground Excavation Vehicle

Kianna Cyr and Jonas Quinn

FALLOUT

Following his return to Kelowna, Jonas continued his naquadria research with Kianna Cyr, a young scientist who had unknowingly been taken as a Goa'uld host. Together they discovered that a chain reaction deep underground was converting naquadah into naquadria and threatening to obliterate the planet.

A manned deep underground excavation vehicle was used to trigger a nuclear explosion near a fault line and isolate the advancing naquadria vein, eliminating the threat to the planet.

The creatures are probably native to Earth, but cannot be seen in our dimension.

AS SG-1 DEALT WITH the loss of Daniel Jackson, Jonas Quinn was welcomed as a new member of the team. From Area 51 came Prometheus, Earth's first interstellar ship, and diplomatic relations with new allies brought valuable new resources: naquadria from Kelowna, tretonin from Pangar, and technology from worlds such as Hebridan and Tagrea. Meanwhile, however, Anubis had dominated the System Lords and stood poised to conquer the galaxy.

PANGAR

A symbiote queen preserved in stasis had been revived and bred by the Pangarans to develop tretonin, a miracle drug that grants perfect health. However, due to a genetic flaw, the drug also caused a dependency, and the realization that the symbiote queen was Egeria, the founder of the Tok'ra, reinforced the ethical dilemma of tretonin production. In a final act of compassion before her death, Egeria herself provided the solution to correct the flawed drug and save the Pangaran people.

The Pangarans have shared tretonin with Earth.

INTER-DIMENSIONAL BEINGS

A device of Ancient design was discovered among the ruins of P9X-391 and brought back to Earth. Activated by touch, it broadcast an energy charge which triggered an ability to see creatures that exist in a dimension parallel to ours. The charge could be passed from person to person by touch, resulting in civilian panic as individuals acquired the ability to see creatures which resemble enormous insects. By rearranging the configuration of the crystals in the device, the effect was reversed, making the inter-dimensional beings invisible again.

PARADISE

Long ago, the Furlings formed a small, secret utopian community and welcomed others from across the galaxy to join them. A deserted temple on P5X-777 was the doorway designed to transport visitors to the paradise on the planet's moon. When O'Neill and Maybourne were transported there, they discovered deserted ruins and evidence that the inhabitants had been affected by the hallucinogenic properties of a plant and had warred with one another until the entire society had been wiped out.

The moon above P5X-777 was once "Paradise."

The general population began to see inter-dimensional beings.

P3X-367

A great plague had befallen the inhabitants of P3X-367, causing grotesque disfigurement and many deaths. When Nirrti arrived on the planet, she promised a cure but instead renewed her genetic experiments by subjecting the inhabitants to a DNA resequencer. The genetic alterations created powers of telekinesis or telepathy in a few inhabitants such as Wodan and Eggar, but most died from the treatments until the people turned against Nirrti and killed her. The inhabitants plan to use the device to make themselves whole again before destroying it.

The DNA resequencer could manipulate genetics by directly altering human DNA in real time.

Wodan used telekinesis to kill Nirrti.

Earth and Hebridan have opened diplomatic relations.

HEBRIDAN

The Hebridan are human, but they share a racially mixed society with the Serrakin, a humanoid race with a reptilian appearance, who helped to liberate Hebridan from the Goa'uld long ago. SG-1 first encountered the Hebridan when the Seberus, a Hebridan prison ship commanded by Warrick Finn, crashed on P2X-005, and SG-1 assisted Warrick in retaking his ship from the escaped prisoners. SG-1 later visited Hebridan at Warrick's invitation, and Warrick and Carter participated in the space race known as the Loop of Kon Garat.

Warrick Finn and his brother Eamon are Serrakin.

The Tagrean stargate had been buried.

TAGREA

Tagrea, or P3X-744, had been founded and abandoned long ago by Heru'ur. In an act of defiance against a false god, the inhabitants destroyed all historical records and buried their stargate. Tagrea was a world without a history. SG-1 met the Tagreans when the Prometheus was stranded in space due to a hyperdrive malfunction. SG-1 was able to establish diplomatic relations with the Tagreans and to locate the Tagrean stargate to return home.

Despite Commander Kalfas's suspicions, Chairman Ashwan w̶...

Missions: Year 7-8

I N A YEAR OF JOY AND SADNESS, SG-1 celebrated the return of Daniel Jackson to human form, and mourned the loss of Janet Fraiser. General O'Neill took command of the SGC, but evil forces gathered on the horizon. On the barren world of Dakara, the powers of the galaxy would be drawn toward Armageddon.

STROMOS

The *Stromos* was one of three cryogenic ships built to carry the survivors of Talthus to Ardena, but the ship crashed on P2A-347 and the cryogenic compartments began to fail. In desperation, Officer Pharrin used Daniel as a "lifeboat", downloading a dozen souls into his mind. To secure Daniel's restoration, SG-1 promised to repair the ship and save Pharrin's race, but Pharrin's son, Keenin, was among the personalities Daniel carried. By absorbing those souls within himself, Pharrin saved the last of his people.

Over one thousand souls were carried in the stasis chambers of the Stromos.

The link, a direct neural interface, connected each inhabitant to the computer.

P3X-289

The village of P3X-289 was shielded from the poisonous atmosphere by a domed force field. A computer network maintained the dome and monitored the population, but as the power supply diminished, the computer compensated by shrinking the dome and eliminating random inhabitants. When the computer link was severed, the inhabitants became aware of the fate of their village, and agreed to relocate to a new homeworld.

SG-1 persuaded Pallan to reprogram the computer link.

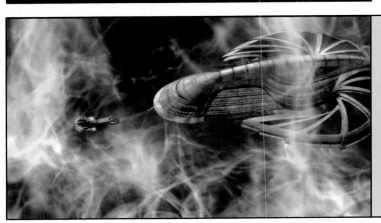

GRACE

Struggling against the effects of a concussion, Carter was visited by an enigmatic young girl named Grace, the embodiment of childlike possibilities, who appeared as a figment of her own mind and guided her to the solution that would allow her to free the *Prometheus* from the cloud in which it had been trapped.

Under attack from an unknown alien vessel, Prometheus *took cover within a nebula-like gas cloud.*

PLANT OF P6J-908

An especially prolific plant from P6J-908 had overwhelmed the SGC, and within two days even a machete and a blow torch had had minimal success at keeping it at bay. By the third day it had cut off all power to the control systems until a strong level of gamma radiation provided a solution for the infestation and eradicated the plant.

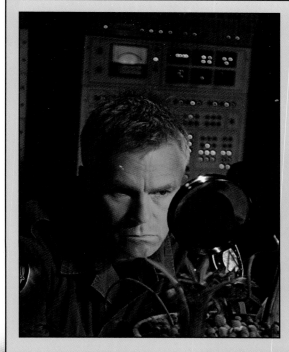

The alien plant was seen as a potential means of solving world hunger until it infiltrated the entire facility.

AVIDAN

The Rand Protectorate and the Caledonian Federation had been locked in a state of cold war for decades, but SG-1's arrival through the stargate prompted religious fundamentalists to return to the ancient beliefs, and uprisings under the leadership of the zealot Soren plunged the planet into global war. Soren named his new nation "Avidan," which means "The Gods Are Just."

SG-1 joined Jared Kane's loyalists in defeating Soren's rebels, and the nations began the long task of rebuilding.

VALA MAL DORAN

During the *Prometheus* expedition to Atlantis, the ship was hijacked by Vala Mal Doran. She insisted that the stolen ship was the only hope to save the last of her people from the Goa'uld, but instead she used the vessel to arrange a rendezvous for the purpose of trading smuggled goods.

Vala left the entire crew, apart from Daniel, on her disabled ship while she hijacked the Prometheus. Eventually the Prometheus was recovered but Vala eluded custody and escaped.

Dakara

DAKARA HAD ONCE been a home of the Ancients, the site from which the powerful race had recreated life in the Milky Way galaxy. Long since abandoned, the planet had become a holy site to both the Goa'uld and the Jaffa, but after thousands of years an enormous temple concealing a device of immense power stood on a largely barren and deserted world. Here the Goa'uld, the Rebel Jaffa, the Replicators, and the Tauri converged, and the Ancient secret of Dakara would determine the fate of the galaxy.

REPLICATOR CARTER

In pursuit of galactic domination, Replicator Carter captured Daniel and reached inside his mind to unlock the knowledge of the Ancients buried there. As she probed his subconscious, she controlled the army of Replicators with her mind, sending them through Earth's stargate and launching a fleet of motherships against the forces of the Goa'uld and Rebel Jaffa at Dakara. However, as she reached into Daniel's mind, he learned how to reach inside hers, to access the Ancient knowledge and the link to Replicators throughout the galaxy.

Mind Probe

Replicator Carter

REBEL JAFFA

The Rebel Jaffa viewed Dakara as a symbol of slavery to the Goa'uld, and Teal'c and Bra'tac devised a plan to seize the planet to prove that the Goa'uld do not possess the power of the gods. Many Jaffa lost their lives in battle against the Goa'uld and the Replicators, but those who survived vowed to build a new Jaffa nation upon the ruins of the holy ground, a haven for all Jaffa who have chosen freedom.

Tolok led the Rebel Jaffa on Dakara.

THE ULTIMATE BATTLE

As Teal'c led the Rebel Jaffa fleet against the Replicator ships above Dakara, O'Neill battled the invasion of Replicators on Earth, and Carter, Jacob, and Ba'al formed an unlikely alliance to unlock the secrets of Dakara's Ancient weapon. Through Replicator Carter, Daniel gained control of the vast armies of Replicators, and for only a few moments, every Replicator in the galaxy was held suspended by the power of Daniel's mind. It cost him his life, as Replicator Carter stabbed Daniel in the heart to release his grip, but in those moments Carter and Jacob modified the Ancient device.

The ultimate battle raged across the galaxy..

ANCIENT WEAPON

The device had been built by the Ancients to create life by first reducing all matter to its basic molecular elements. Similar in design to disruptor technology, it held the key to eliminating the Replicators. Carter and Jacob succeeded in recalibrating the device and the weapon was activated. With Ba'al's assistance the energy wave translated through every stargate in the galaxy simultaneously. Replicator Carter and her vast army were instantly and completely disintegrated into harmless inert blocks.

The Ancient weapon rose from Dakara's temple.

An energy wave destroyed every Replicator in the galaxy.

ANUBIS

As part of his grand design, Anubis intended to seize Dakara's Ancient weapon to obliterate all life in the galaxy and to repopulate it to his own specifications. Following the destruction of the Replicators, the Rebel Jaffa claimed Dakara as their new homeworld, but their forces soon fell to Anubis who retook the planet and prepared to activate the weapon. It was Oma Desala who intervened. Suddenly, Anubis vanished, locked in eternal battle on a higher plane, leaving his forces to be vanquished. The galaxy was spared.

Anubis faced Oma Desala in battle for eternity.

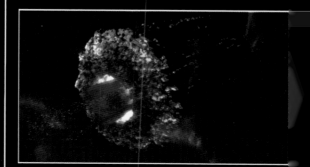

Replicator Carter's ship was instantly disintegrated.

Moebius

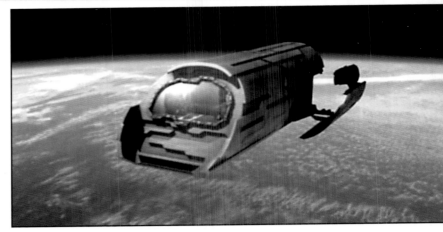

ANCIENT TECHNOLOGY had made time travel possible but had not eliminated the danger of adversely affecting the timeline. However, when evidence suggested the presence of a ZPM on Earth during the reign of Ra, the opportunity to acquire a device that would power Earth's defenses and allow stargate travel to the Pegasus galaxy was deemed worth the risk. Using the power of his mind, O'Neill successfully piloted the Ancient spacecraft through time, instantly sending SG-1 to Egypt in the year 3000 BC.

An Ancient spacecraft and time travel device had been recovered from Maybourne's planet.

EGYPT 3000 BC

The plan to steal the ZPM from Ra's temple worked flawlessly, however SG-1 was unable to return to the present without altering the future. Forced to remain in the past, the team was drawn into a spiral of events that would play out exactly as they were meant to. In a tomb, SG-1 concealed the ZPM and a video recording that described their mission, the future world they had left behind, and the absence of fish in O'Neill's pond.

SG-1 acquired a functioning ZPM from Ra's temple.

REBELLION

Despite the risk of changing history, SG-1 made the decision to become involved in the rebellion that they knew would overthrow Ra. But when their plans were exposed, O'Neill, Carter, and Teal'c were captured and executed. Daniel worked to build a second underground movement, and in 2995 BC, the Egyptians rose up against their god. The rebellion succeeded, Earth was freed, and Ra abandoned the planet. However, he took the stargate with him.

The rebellion against Ra liberated Earth from the Goa'uld but changed history.

SG-1 remained in the past and helped orchestrate the rebellion against Ra.

ALTERNATE TIMELINE

The rebellion in Egypt set into motion an alternate timeline in which the Stargate Program never existed. When a ZPM, tablet, and video camera were discovered in an Egyptian tomb, they were sent to Cheyenne Mountain for study, and the Air Force summoned Carter, Daniel, and O'Neill. The artifacts proved that history had changed and provided the key to locating the Antarctic stargate, and O'Neill led a seven-man team to Chulak in search of Teal'c.

Civilians Daniel and Carter attempted to persuade O'Neill to come out of retirement.

CHULAK

On Chulak, the team was captured by Jaffa, and Daniel was brought before Apophis and implanted with a Goa'uld symbiote. Persuaded by words of freedom, Teal'c helped the prisoners escape, but only O'Neill, Carter, and Teal'c survived to make their escape in the spacecraft as they returned to Egypt 5000 years in the past.

Teal'c was persuaded to betray his god and helped the team to escape.

EGYPT 2995 BC

In 2995 BC, just as history was meant to be, O'Neill, Carter, and Teal'c met Daniel from the original team and led the rebellion against Ra that freed Earth from the Goa'uld. The stargate was buried in Giza where it would be found 5000 years later.

THE CIRCLE IS COMPLETE

This time, when the ZPM and video artifacts were brought to the SGC, the facts on the tape coincided with the current timeline, and the team retired to O'Neill's cabin, with a pond full of fish. Close enough.

With Katep, the team devised a plan to capture the stargate.

A S THE NINTH YEAR of the Stargate Program began, General O'Neill had been reassigned, and with Carter at Area 51, Daniel departing for Atlantis, and Teal'c a leader of the new Jaffa nation, the elite team of SG-1 had been disbanded. On the horizon, however, lay an enemy more ominous than any they had encountered before, a race of evil ascended beings known as the Ori.

LIEUTENANT COLONEL CAMERON MITCHELL

An outstanding leader and pilot, Cameron Mitchell had led the dogfight against Anubis's forces in Antarctica. He was critically wounded when his F-302 was shot down, but his heroism had earned him the respect of O'Neill, who promised him his choice of any posting at the SGC. Wanting to work with the best, Mitchell requested a position on SG-1, and he made it his goal to reunite the flagship team, to recruit Carter, Daniel, and Teal'c, and to "get the band back together."

VALA MAL DORAN

Once a host to the Goa'uld Qetesh, Vala had been freed from her symbiote and made her way as a trader and smuggler. Resourceful, unscrupulous, and relentlessly flirtatious, she came to Earth seeking incredible buried treasures, but as the Ori prepared a beachhead in this galaxy, Vala risked her life to prevent the formation of a supergate, and was drawn into the Ori galaxy. There she became a pawn in the Ori crusade, carrying a child that would be the "will of the Ori."

THE ORI

Long ago, the Alterans were one society, but a philosophical division grew. Those who left their galaxy for Avalon came to be known as the Ancients, while those who remained behind were the Ori. Both eventually ascended, but the Ancients believed in free will, whereas the Ori passed down the religion of Origin to their followers. Although the Ori promise enlightenment, they instead empower themselves by sapping the life force of the millions of humans who relinquish their free will to worship them.

THE PRIORS

In the City of the Gods on Celestis burn the Flames of Enlightenment, the embodiment of the ascended Ori. Their followers look for guidance to the Priors, humans who have been transformed by the Ori's powers. As priests or missionaries, the ghostly Priors are charged with spreading the word of Origin and bringing retribution to unbelievers. When the Ori learned of humans in our galaxy, the Priors were sent forth, and dozens of worlds were forced to embrace Origin or be obliterated by devastation or pestilence.

Landry's daughter, Dr. Carolyn Lam, became the SGC's new Chief Medical Officer.

MAJOR GENERAL HANK LANDRY

General O'Neill had personally selected his longtime friend, Hank Landry, as his successor at the SGC. O'Neill's reassignment and promotion to major general had taken him from Cheyenne Mountain, and he considered General Landry "the best of the best," the most qualified to command in his place. A strong leader, shrewd negotiator, and keen judge of human nature, Landry quickly earned the respect of those at the SGC and insisted that "a general is only as good as the people he commands."

DAY OF RECKONING

The Priors were the harbingers of the final battle between the light and darkness when the Ori would come to defeat the Ancients. Huge ships and vast armies prepared for the crusade that would destroy all unbelievers. A micro-singularity and a massive supergate created a wormhole between galaxies, and four Ori ships entered our galaxy. The Day of Reckoning had arrived, when all who have renounced the Ori will feel their wrath.

Index

LONDON, NEW YORK, MUNICH,
MELBOURNE, AND DELHI

Senior Editor Lindsay Kent **Senior Designer** Nathan Martin
Publishing Manager Simon Beecroft **Designer** Dan Newman
Category Publisher Alex Allan **Brand Manager** Rob Perry
Production Nick Seston **DTP Design** Hanna Ländin

First American edition, 2006
07 08 09 10 9 8 7 6 5 4 3
Published in the United States by DK Publishing
375 Hudson Street, New York, New York 10014

Based on the television series developed by Brad Wright & Jonathan Glassner.

Published in Great Britain by Dorling Kindersley Limited.

A catalog record for this book is available from the Library of Congress.

ISBN-13: 978-0-7566-2361-6
ISBN-10: 0-7566-2361-8

Reproduced by Media Development and Printing Ltd., UK
Leo Paper Products Ltd., China

ACKNOWLEDGMENTS

The publisher would like to thank the following people: Stephen Bahr for help with visual effects; Paul Brown at Legends Memorabilia for supplying props;
Richard Chasemore for producing the illustrations on pages 56–57 and page 93; Kawoosh! Productions IX Inc. for photographing props; Jon Rosenberg and
Karol Mora at MGM for all their help; James Robbins for his invaluable advice.

The author would like to thank the following people: Thomasina Gibson for seeing potential, Brigitte Prochaska, Barry Peters, Susan Pajos, Kenny
Gibbs, Jan Newman, James Robbins, and Douglas Thar for their assistance and expertise, Paul Brown for his support and generosity, Peter DeLuise for his
encouragement and limitless knowledge, and Richard Dean Anderson for his inspiration.

MGM would like to thank the following people: Kate Ritter for her dedication to Stargate SG-1; Producers Brad Wright and Robert C. Cooper;
Richard Dean Anderson; Amanda Tapping; Michael Shanks; Chris Judge; Ben Browder; Beau Bridges; Brigitte Prochaska and Carole Appleby; James Robbins
and Jennifer Kidd; Paul Brown; Stephen Bahr; Doug Thar; the entire cast and crew of Stargate SG-1.

Discover more at

www.dk.com